ANTHEM

ISBN: 978-0-9843991-7-8

Printed in the United States of America.

Cover design by LTP Creative.

SAGE HILL RESOURCES

624 Grassmere Park Drive, Suite 11
Nashville, TN 37211
www.sagehillresources.com

THE REASON FOR
ANTHEM

——

I write this letter to you in the year 87 AC (After Collapse). The Doctor, whom you no doubt have heard of and will read about later in the story, urged me to write. He asked all of the people intimately involved in establishing a shifted society to communicate the experience: where we were, what happened, and what we did that brought us to living again and loving more deeply.

We all knew that those who came after us would quickly forget the past. However, I do not write this story so we do not repeat the past; we do not want the past to block us from our future. A memorable thinker said, "When experience is not retained ... infancy is perpetual." We want to grow, so we remember.

This story is but a slice of the whole picture, so the assimilation of the many histories from other regions around the earth will give us the larger story. The call to create an anthology went out to the communities all over the earth. The Doctor hoped that the anthology could be completed before his passing. It wasn't, but we have finished it. The final anthology edition is expected in 88 AC.

After the Collapse, groups of the greatest minds and experience formed the Collective. Its purpose was to create the greatest good for the greatest number after society collapsed from its own "boundary-less" connective weight. The vision of the Collective was O% deficit of human fulfillment. Everyone was thrilled or at least involved. We hoped we had avoided a cataclysm. Not until later did we realize that the Collective had already been prepared to step into the breach when our world came apart; they even prepped us for it through our pain. They waited until our intolerance for dis-ease outweighed the heart of relationship. (This sentence will make more sense later in the story).

The Collective took over the world; we gave it to them. I worked for the Collective. I had been trained to say "with" the Collective, but it wasn't true; I was a tool of a premeditated system. The Collective created order and peace—and mechanistic sterility of living. The ideal of the greatest good for the greatest number led to the rejection of individual thought and powerfully seductive suppression was the result. The heart of humanity essentially was "cut out" in the name of peace. We had even pleaded for it! And I had been brought in to help make it all effective, efficient, and to keep it pure.

The Collective worked. We had less strife, and yet decreased potency. More goods and yet more disappearances; more organization and less time for relationship. Our peace had become a uniformity of expression. Our freedom had become a prison.

What happened to push us to sacrifice liberty? Simply put, the material-biological world and the spiritual world of humanity had collided. The evolution of technological movements, humanity's lust to avoid pain, biological mutations, and denial had slammed together with grotesque results because we gave up what makes us human—the heart of who we are and the heart of who we are to become.

The story that follows is true. Those of you in our community who read it have progressed far enough to forget. But please don't. I am old now. I once was young like you, and my heart beat the same as yours. Let that kinship give you relationship with this story and with us who have gone before you. It speaks of our own awakening, my own return to what I had left behind, and the heartbeat of what living again means.

I hope this story, your story, will continue the fire that was set in the hearts of liberty, and grow the blaze. It is an anthem to you. It is our anthem. After the story, I leave you with a message of love—The War of Love. For you who have the heart to grasp the message, live it well. We shall never be defeated. The war continues until the Invisible becomes visible.

Keep Heart,
Abe

I

―――――

The sun rose and fell again. The color of day faded. I could hear the rustling of wrens near the house, nesting in a hanging basket of ivy along the wall of the back porch. Night settled in without event; the moonlight and shadows turned everything outside to shades of black and gray. Water coming out of the spout in the holding tank near our courtyard sparkled in the moonlight. The sound reminded me of hot summers and warm springs, cut grass, the grill lit, watering the plants, finishing the day and joining together.

We turned the lights in the house up when the room inside became too dark to read. I could hear the crickets outside. A moth tapped gently on the glass of a window, only inches from three candles that smelled like bees wax and honeysuckle as they melted down to clear liquid. In the quiet I heard a barn owl screech once. It sheltered itself and its young ones in the crook of a cedar where lightning had struck years before. A splintered limb still hung by twisted sinews near the trunk twenty feet from the ground; its branches stuck in the ground where brown cedar prongs still clung to the limbs. I left it just like it fell when I saw the nest.

I sat at one end of our aging leather couch; one leg extended toward her and one foot rested on the Persian rug. I read the end of *Monte Cristo* again, the last chapter, the letter and the wisdom, and then the last sentence—to remind me to keep my heart awake and the gear shift of my actions and attitude in forward or neutral. No reverse. I had many, many paragraphs to remind me.

Closing the thick volume, placing it on an end table of other books, I passed my eyes around our keeping room. The cast bronze of the Seed Thrower sat on a table; in front of it a blue glass water bottle now filled with volcanic dirt from Mt. Aetna, a jar of rocks and sea glass from Mykonos, oil lamps from the Davidic period of Israel we uncovered on an archeological dig, gifted to us by the director. On the shelves a volume of pressed flowers from the region of Tuscany, a light green and gray sea stone from Trunk Bay, photos of places, events, travels, all markers of what reminded us to remember. I smiled, looking at the shot of Beatrice blowing snow from her mouth after a ski fall while in the Appalachians. Books and books, and memory treasures—a small bag of acorns, wheat seeds, small items of ancient jewelry, starfish, conch shells, a rosewood cross and a bird nest shaped like a heart that I had found when clearing a thicket one fall.

The walls were covered with paintings, journey maps of ancient explorations, and tapestries, one a silk tapestry from Turkey in the region of Ephesus, a butterfly collection, and a large print of *The Creation of Adam* by Michelangelo. An overhead light highlighted the gap between the reaching hand of the Creator and the outstretched hand of humanity; that was the place of the room where I cast my visual net. Every object symbolized memories and stories, experiences and our lives with friends and our sons. Above our mantel hung a large framed photo of a path shrouded by hemlocks, stones glistening in the morning dew and fog blocking the view down the path beyond a certain distance. Our youngest son had taken it on his way down Mt. Leconte years ago; a black and white photo that in its starkness highlighted the mystery of what he walked into, which I took for what we all walk into unless we stay where we are. Even if we stay where we are, the path and fog eventually come to us.

My eyes rested on Bea. Her reading glasses rested on her nose as she focused on papers in her lap, her salt and pepper hair pushed behind her ear. Her profile, "absolutely perfect" a plastic surgeon once told me at a party; "the perfect nose," he said. I drifted into a warm trance of watching her. Tenderness welled up inside me when I watched her, and admiration; such memories of the fight to have her. Not one regret, considering all that makes life yield its worth to us. Choice becomes easy that way. I had far too long relied on my intellectual training and ambition to achieve a better world, and almost missed the life I was destined to have. I had been so blinded by my own research, even though it was accurate and meaningful.

She looked up, feeling me watching her. I marvel at how our brains move with the heart's intuition more fruitfully than with what we think we know. Her olive eyes rested softly on my face, then on my eyes. I swear the expression came into me for a moment. Her lips turned up just at the corners, smiling slightly, but not breaking her concentration. I can read her lips to see her mood, yet her eyes I travel and never come to the end.

When she finished her work, I turned down the lights, and blew out the candles, the wax completely clear in the pans where the wicks burned low. I heard a wind chime outside the windows catch a breeze, ringing twice before falling silent again.

As she washed her face in the stand-up sink, I lay in bed, already sleepy. I liked the familiar sound of the squeaking faucet handle turning off. The mundane had become a treasure, and I liked old things that had lost value unless someone wise knew to see them and reclaim them.

A piece of a poem drifted into my floating thoughts. I had found it on the back of an envelope that had been folded in half, crumpled, then pitched. It was in the corner of the front room of an old abandoned house. Handwritten in cursive, 40 years old when I found it. I remembered the lines because I wished that whomever had written them could have been a neighbor, and we could have known them just like that poem.

Bea walked from the sink with a white cotton gown,

showing the silhouette of her form underneath it as she turned the light down by the sink and walked barefoot to our bed. The words of the writing rolled through my memory of paragraphs.

Stars shine upon the crest of the hill
Each alone a diamond on black,
Soft breeze blows caressingly about,
Whispering mystery only few may know.
Sounds of the gentle night play
Smoothly upon those who hear.
A solitary tree stands old and strong,
Holding time upon gnarled arms with grace.
They wander beneath the marker of time,
Stopping now to touch the night.
A single leaf drifts downward slowly,
Landing near them noticed.
The breeze lifts eyes that meet,
And the night sings quietly in their minds.

I remembered the last two lines were scratched through, even though I liked them most.

I understood them finally, knew them to be true. Since I saw those thoughts, I remembered them like one of the paragraphs of truths. All the paragraphs reminded me; I have watched more and listened more, I have seen more and heard more until it all had become seeing and hearing behind things. I had run away as far as I could. The rest of my time, I would live in love.

Beatrice slid under the covers after lighting a candle, and I pulled the sheet up to the edge of her shoulders. I laid on my right side, arm tucked under my pillow. She lay on her left side. I brushed her hair away from her cheek. I lay within 12 inches of her face. We looked into each other's eyes. The olive pools told stories. She reached out and followed the four parallel scars on my shoulder down my arm, then pulled her hand back under the sheet. We spoke not a word. Her eyes became heavy, as did mine. Not one word, better than a dream and a hundred paragraphs. I remembered her eyes shutting in sleep just before mine.

Those minutes were the best minutes of my life. Sometimes I think they are actually the paragraphs.

II

L ate into the night, as had become our routine, I would get up, and ease from the room quietly to dress. Bea would barely stir since she was so used to the ritual. After I finished the hunt, she would be waiting for me as the sun came up. We had been hunting for years by that time, and the scars of it went deeper than my torn flesh.

I always walked into the woods with slow methodical steps, careful to find the hole by feel, being quite careful not to slip; the last time I fell and crashed through the dark, I barely escaped with my throat intact. The scars on my shoulder and back healed slowly, toxins battled to envelope my skin and my insides. I learned much. From then onward, I hunted on the late side of midnight, always after 2:30 and before 4:00 a.m. They isolated then, a habit of necessity, and could be caught in a lull, though never asleep.

I wore a double-layered leather-sleeved tunic, cinched by a belt. On my left arm from elbow to wrist, a leather guard covered my forearm down to the knuckles and was tied at the blood side of my wrist. On the sides of my tunic were stirrups sewn below the belt, and on my back was a large pouch, sewn on to be able to carry whoever I could release. My canvas pants fit loosely from rarely being washed except in the holding tank. Dirt and leather was the scent. I also wore a steel blade, 14 inches from tip to handle end, razor sharp down each side and a leather scabbard hung on the front of my belt, just over the thigh of my left hip.

My boots had soft, thick leather bottoms, and were laced tightly up my shins. They fit snugly and let me run hard and move quickly as I felt the earth's contours beneath my feet. I had a leather guard around my neck and a leather helmet pulled over my head, forehead and the bridge of my nose, with jut-outs that guarded my cheekbones. My ears were not covered. I needed hearing and scent as much as eyes to be weapons, and yet these weapons remained vulnerable to the worst wounds. My senses had become like my quickness, my strength, and my love. The attacks did not concern me as much as what happened if I get trapped. I wanted to live and serve, not just survive.

At 3:00 a.m. this night, the darkness lies black on black. No moon; no lightning. All but the most nocturnal creatures were still. Outlines above ground made discerning substance without some light nearly impossible. Underground, 3:00 a.m. made the darkness even darker and me that much more prepared for it. I had only been caught once. I had time for one save a night. I have had seven in a week, but the strain creates danger because of weakness, and if I'm not fully prepared, the potentials would get me killed. I had no more than one hour tops, to search, find, and be out. Other searchers were out there. We did not suffer this alone, but we had to search on our own. That procedure was the only one that worked. The spirituality of desire and the limbic power of dyadic relationship simply constrains any other way.

Walking slowly near the trunks along the root paths of the largest trees, I felt the bark for brittle qualities and the leaves for dryness, the effects of dehydration. I felt along the ground for divot-like scars in the ground or soft dirt the way moles leave results of underground activity. The openings that I uncovered were man-sized, as much for the guts of the creature as the shoulders.

Once I found a hole, my heart rate climbed. I breathed quietly to still myself, until the anger of hunting for life prepared me to go into the deeper dark. I went in feet first, hanging by my hands on roots, just below the surface, and felt for the sides of the tunnel with my boots. Once I got the bearings of the tunnel, I dropped into the dark, letting go completely while landing somewhere between 10 to 12 feet below ground on soft churned dirt. The deepest drop was never more than 12 feet if my guess is correct, and I could hang to roots on the way down, but the dark could make the drop full of dread. I also bear the scars of not being prepared.

The smell of the earth filled my nostrils, reminding me of a prepped construction site or upturned soil in a field. Sometimes the scent was of maple wood and dirt, sassafras or oak and dirt. Each tree has its own distinct scent. The roots were always scarred, and I could feel fresh woodcuts in the roots below ground. I don't know if they drew food from the roots or just sharpened their claws and teeth, or both. For whatever purpose, I was certain that the root site was the only place that necessitated a gathering of these extremely isolated creatures.

I hit flat ground, would bend low for many steps forward and then stand in a crouched fighting position as the tunnels widen and become higher and roomier, making burrow-like rooms and larger open spaces. The clods of dirt under my feet squished quietly. All my senses lit up on ready. I looked for the first glimpse of the dim flicker of eyes with the slightest glimmer of light. They were always isolated at this time, unless alarm created a frenzy of blind attacks. Not so in early night.

I saw light flicker for a split second and charged as quickly as my might allowed. The dagger came out in my right hand, sliding smoothly out of the oiled leather. I ran right at the eyes, estimating in the dark 28 inches below the last sight of light. Before it could turn, shut its eyes to hide, or squeal its pig-like snarl, I would slam my left forearm into its throat, pushing it into the wall. The squeal could kick off the chaos of a wasp nest that had been hit if I didn't land my first blow perfectly. I had to avoid their screams to avoid them. When one lets out a wail, the whole burrow became tormenting.

I had to stay in front, not rolling to either side, cutting off the airway quickly to block sound. In the same movement, I buried the dagger seven inches into its gut and sliced upwards with all my guided fury, cutting through coarse hair, tough hide covered by flinty scales, into sinewy thick muscles, thin bones and phosphorescent entrails. I moved the blade up hard and fast, gutting the creature up to the bottom of the sternum, surgeon-like, stopping just before the point my blade would nick the heart. If I hit it, we lost; the imprisoned died an agonizing, slow, though merciful death, and I carried death home.

If I struck well, no air came out of the throat at all, no sound but the flatulence of stench and the ooze of guts from the bowels that cover the dirt, my pants, and boots. I released the throat, grabbed the loose scales and hair about the neck, and pulled the foul creature within an inch of my mouth, saying with whispered urgency, "You listen to me. I saw your eyes. I know you're in there. I'm going to let you go. I'm headed out fast. Follow the phosphorescence of my steps that came from your oozing gut. As soon as it fades, feel for the imprints of my steps. I will wait at the edge of the tunnel where the dirt and wood smell is. I will pull you out. You have minutes before I have to go. If you get there, I can save you. Then we must run. I will carry you."

As soon as one reached the edge of the hole, the gray light of darkness outlined the outstretched clawed hands that reached toward the opening. I would wait with quick deep breathing for this last, most difficult moment. I reached to the paws swiftly, careful not to slice my hands on its razor sharp claws, and drag the creature out. Reaching into the empty spaces where I stabbed deeply into the hairy scales, I would bring my arms around the body of skin inside the creature's opened gut, and put my hands on the shoulder blades while standing on the feet of the creature. I pulled the created towards my chest, then leaned my left shoulder into the guts and pushed upward against the sternum of the creature's carcass. I then birthed the imprisoned life, pulling it into my arms. The stench and fluid of electric sewage and phosphorescent fuel would cover my clothes and arms, my neck and face. It burned the skin on my hands and where it touched any skin on my face or ears. If I got that far, the risk of being poisoned all but diminished unless I had been cut during the rescue. Then, I would have to wait to see if my very being would become trapped in the poisonous suspension of paralysis, of a painful vision out of the eyes of a creature that literally drained the life out of the heart of the one who had been transmuted. Tortured to see; poisoned to kill. Sucking from the heart of life for survival.

The carcass would fall slowly to my feet, still supported by thick muscle, sinew and bones. Pulling the head of the created from the face and cartilage of the creature was the most tedious work. Done carelessly, it would pull the created's skin completely off to the bone, making survival impossible. Finally, I would free the living being from the carcass, grab the created and carefully, yet awkwardly, slide the emaciated form of whomever I had birthed into the pouch on my tunic and pull their ankles toward the stirrups. I would tell them to hold on to me if they could. Usually I would hear a gasp of grunting relief as the full weight of them came to rest in the pouch, arms around my shoulders if they could hang on. Most of the time they simply could not.

Then, I ran. I ran hard as a horse trained to carry its master to war. I ran in the starlight or lightening-streaked darkness, moonlight or pitch black. I ran the way I came, home to the dawn of day, hoping I could get the created back in time to stop more damage from the burning of acid that had met the air.

If I could make it, they all became beautiful at dawn. We soaked them in the holding tank of clean warm water that came from our spring; Bea and I had rigged a heater tank that warmed the water and a circulator that filtered the water throughout the whole process of cleansing. We mixed aloe and eucalyptus through the water to cool the burned skin and opened the lungs to life again. Our holding pool was almost like sitting in a dammed area of a warm creek that stills the water flow for a time and then rushes on. If I could reach home in time, the burns from the acid didn't reach so deeply and spread so far; the breathing improved quickly in the cleansing pool. Beatrice was always waiting and ready. We washed the flotsam and jetsam from their created skin, and never stopped marveling when the sun came over the horizon and the light touched the rebirth.

Bea loved when we got one home safely. She loved my return. She was given way completely, long before I woke up and finally went home.

III

L ong before I became a hunter, I had been a renowned
academic social philologist. Long before I really knew
what love cost, I had been an intellectual expert on relational
and community peace. I had been part of the Collective.
And I still feel the regret when I remember.

The night the change began was at my last Collective
Conference. It had been coming for years for me, but I still
shocked myself by doing what I would have historically
called giving up or quitting. I left the Collective. I didn't decide to change with a direction; I just knew I couldn't continue. I cast all to the destiny of what I didn't know. What I
found was the rest of me.

I had crafted an extremely well researched and
multi-disciplinary paper to identify the philological erosion
and loss of accurate meaning that occurs when etymology
is sacrificed to present cultural demands. As a social philologist, my integrity required holding the line, so to speak,
in the historical accuracy of words, a way for cultures to remain ontologically connected, and true to recognized ideals. As a philologist, I had unearthed a clear thread of proof

of words' power to keep us true to clarity of direction or divert us from our course, as I had been hired to warn against. The Collective had sought me out to be a part of correcting course, to be a watchdog for our societies. I hoped that the offer had verity of purpose; I, even with my doubts, still saw no other way to affect change. The money had enticed me, for sure, as well as the prestige. Even more, though, having an influence pushed me to offer my hard won gifts.

All of my research had led me to Milton, the bulwark heart, blind poet and visionary prophet. I noted that he had pointed very directly to the place at which we would lose direction and cast away from our moorings to the truths of the human heart and creation created. Who Shakespeare had been to the earth and relationships' depths and twists, loves and losses, Milton had been the polar equal to the universe, the cosmic interactions and their movements among humankind for the very sake of each person. Without Milton, Shakespeare loses love; without Shakespeare, Milton's love remains too powerful for human touch. Milton had shown us how to grasp and keep ourselves intact for life's fullness and mystery. I was to reveal the discoveries to the Collective the night the scales fell from my eyes. I saw what I had dared not feel. In my hope, I had been led astray myself. I had mistaken martyrdom for heroism and true heroism as a part of a child's past.

I expected the Collective to use what they had sought me out to do, which would require introspection and courage within the powers they held. Five other presenters from around the world expected the same. The baseline foundational recognition of academia's departure from baseline foundational etymological acceptance had ramifications for all academic disciplines, and, therefore, for the maintenance of the stability of culture, across a continuous span, from morality to economics, from relational intimacy to the art of engineering principles. The opportunity for academic systems to identify forms of departure and begin reintegrating an objective agenda was as great an opportunity as the ancient church once had to welcome Galileo, or open a door to Newton.

Now was the time for academia and society, at large, to offer itself to continued discovery while working from a context of certainty. While others, myself included, were considered mavericks in our fields, I feared that somehow our research and reports would not create change or a difference. In fact, all of our previous reports had gone to the foggy sink of committee over and again. Our daring proposals continuously went into delay, even though we were solicited to create change and paid very well by the Collective. I feared the Collective would cling to Aristotle to the exclusion of mystery, an ancient problem, one that set the course of persecution by the early church upon those who plumbed mystery. Was the Collective going to repeat the problem, the mission of the Collective being to ensure that nothing as such would ever happen again, the best for everyone?

With the triune brain research of the past decades, I

assumed a readiness to consider that the heart, now referred to by science as the limbic system, carries verities of humanity across culture and vertically throughout history. Facial expressions indicate affective consistencies and similarities, under related occurrences, i.e., fright looks like what we assume, as does the anguish of loss in sadness, as does the responsiveness to pain of wounds in hurt. Humans, unlike all other animated life, had the capability of committing great error, even evil through the capacity to refuse or withhold internal experience that makes us known to others and ourselves. We can use our faces to hide our internal experiences. This refusal blocks opportunity for identification of humanity's kinship, establishes walls rather than boundaries, and sets humans up for multiple forms of isolation, the antipathy of being human. My reach for kinship, using multiple learning disciplines, sound reasoning, scientific research, and history had elucidated truths that spurred no interest in the very group that had initially brought me into the Collective. The deeper the truths I discovered, the more I saw, the more diminished I became and the less they heard. Frankly, it was crazy. The Collective's power of refusal in the name of unity of all culture was rejecting the very reasoned and passion-based reality before them.

At the conference where I presented my findings, the other five presenters were also given forty-eight minutes to communicate their findings. We would go long into the night. I connected thoroughly to their work, the tedious focus, and the hope that we would make a difference this night. Experts from around the six academic regions of the Americas were present. Panels of discussion began as soon as the reader completed their work. A member of each region had been chosen by the president of the regions to oversee the discussions. Quite an honor and a vitae achievement. The panel leaders would be able to go anywhere in the Collective they chose after the conference and follow any interest the Collective had listed as its primary concerns.

Four presenters had completed their work to expected, well-deserved, and sadly, obligatory applause from the regional panelists, host members and audience of one hundred and eighty experts. I listened closely to the panel discussions, thirty minutes in length, including audience participation. To my dismay, the panel members did not actually discuss anything that had been presented at the podium. The lead panelist glanced down at prescribed notes.

They had not written a single word during the readings. I began to watch closely after the second presenter. The last three panel leaders spoke from prepared questions, occasionally glancing down at their notes, memorized ahead of the presenters. I watched one leader appear to rub her forehead while she actually read over her questions before the presenter finished. She checked her notes several times in the same way during the 48 minutes of erudite expression. We, the experts, were invisible.

I stood once to make a comment, even though I was

about to present within the next 10 minutes. I was intending to question a clear disparity between the discussion and the substance of a paper by a colleague who had been raised and educated in what had been known as Japan. She spoke with artistic beauty about post nuclear Japan and a culture that had incrementally descended into a condition called *Karoshi*, death by work, over a period of 200 years in the name of progress and prevention of tragedy. She noted how the condition is more akin to addictive behavior as a reaction to trauma, rather than a logical choice based upon cultural and economic needs. The people had completely suppressed the inborn response to essential emotions or *sentio* and uniformly established the absence of intimacy. She spoke of family dissonance, philological detachment from family, until words lost connection to their own community and subsequent denial led to individual isolation.

She ended with a clarion call from John Donne. I knew Dr. Narohashi well from her works. I also knew the history of her family, the loss of lives and the deterioration of closeness, a connection that had once marked their legacy with intimacy and true productivity of service. It allowed me to grasp the gravity of Narohashi's personal attachment to Donne's words. Tears came to her eyes as she read Donne's line, "Do not ask for whom the bell tolls, it tolls for thee." She felt every loss as her culture faded. The uniform Collective dictates required command over the internal makeup of the human being. They had been ripe for the take over. Safety ruled with the tolerance of an iron fist. Protection sacrificed the best, because the best always brings pain. She believed what she said, spoke articulately, and shared with clear erudition in her field to faceless applause.

No one responded to my comment and question that reflected the pathos with which my colleague spoke. Dr. Narohashi barely held her tongue as she watched the panel. I saw her shift at the podium and squeeze her rolled up paper in her fist. My friend's responsiveness and truthfulness, along with mine, had been completely negated by silence.

IV

––––––

The introduction of my credentials before I presented my paper lasted what seemed like an interminable period of time. At that station in my career, I was known in many academic and social contract-influenced sites around the globe. During that span of minutes, I was flooded within about the separation of reality from the truth. Five speakers had presented profound findings with great depth and humility, at times seeming to plead to be heard. The material wasn't new; rather, it communicated our relationship to ancient consistencies. They all pointed directly to how language had been manipulated to negate verities of the heart. I was up next to become invisible. The recognition of the reality that had been overwhelming me allowed the truth to surface with an experiential voice. I made a decision. My departure lay much less than 48 minutes away by half.

I shortened my paper by half, without a single change. Standing before the group, I looked out into the lights and faces. The hired press took the three photos for use in the year-end clippings and codification records. I finished read-ing the first page and then skipped every other page for the duration of the presentation. Page seven contained the crux and core of the work. The power point rested on Michelangelo's painting from the Sistine Chapel of Creator reaching toward the human and the human reaching toward Creator. The Creator reaches from what is a ventricle of the human heart within which are painted divine images, who direct their attention to the Creator's reach and the human's awakening response to creation.

I left the *imago dei* on the screen. The paper at this juncture introduced Nietzsche's word play on the word indemnity as a form of vengeance used by what was then considered sophisticated, modern society to dictate sameness, or safety through uniformity. This brilliant, yet, incomplete metaphysical philologist railed about how the society that sought uniformity by changing meaning robs those with gifted capacities of glorying in them. Then, I traced how Nietzsche gave a foretelling of how modernity would turn indemnity away from its meaning. The word that once meant protecting people with mercy through compassion so that they could contend fully in the world had become a demand. It became a right to escape life to escape pain. A person demanded to be prevented from experiencing loss in their lives. The Collective used the word to promise as much in a future day. For one to be indemnified, one must placate the "powers that be" with conformity of thought to receive protection. Sameness had begun to triumph as Nietzsche suggested in Chapter VII of *Good and Evil*. This advanced writing was published in 1886 (AD). Nietzsche's words after his death would be abused first by his sister, an anti-Semite, and then as history clearly records, a nation took pieces of his unfinished and very incomplete philosophical rantings that held potential in them. They then turned them to twisted superiority and genocidal holocaust of a people Nietzsche considered the toughest group of people on earth, the Hebrews.

I then moved to the territory of John Milton, perhaps the greatest philologist of all time, to begin to tie kinship connections to writers and thinkers who had historically been held as oppositional in thought to each other, as in Nietzsche and Milton, the former a rabid atheist and the latter an unwavering believer. I reported the story of how Milton had met Galileo on a journey to Italy, where Milton was quite well-known. Galileo had become a prisoner in his own home for searching out the truth from the "not yet realized." Or as Milton would refer years later to the "known not known" in *Paradise Lost* as a statement of support for those who had followed their Creator in the pursuit of elucidating life. I contended that Milton had, like Nietzsche, laid down a confrontation for future generations to remain awake to and contend with: The struggle of heart in a tragic place and the guarding of its core during times and influences in which the courage of hope would seem an archetype of foolishness.

In *Paradise Lost*, Book I, line 108, from Satan's mouth comes the line, "Courage never to submit or yield," and what follows is the proclamation of the power and worship of the Will:

> *What the field be lost?*
> *All is not lost; the unconquerable*
> *Will, And study of revenge, immortal hate,*
> *And courage never to submit or yield.*
> *Lower than Hell is ignomy*
> *And shame beneath this downfall.*

What brilliance Milton had been gifted with to show us the future as the blind poet whose darkness would become the light for our future. In the mouth of Satan, obduracy becomes courage. Self-created humankind versus created humankind will value will-power over heart; whereas, "Will," notably, is to be a servant of the heart. Milton warns that the word 'courage' would be confiscated from its origins to take on a meaning that has contradictory realities; thus, he lets the words come from the mouth of the Deceiver of humanity.

Milton brilliantly shows how this movement pushes the word courage towards the supremacy of Will against life, rather than its true meaning that calls us to live life with heart, and therefore vulnerability, or hope in perseverance. Again, I pointed to how the will of the human being is to be a servant of the emotional and spiritual makeup of the person; as in the old adage from a group from the past, called AA. They noted that the proper place of will was the daily decision to live a spiritual program so that sobriety from alcohol and recovery of life could be guarded. These people had rediscovered the emptiness of self-will when used to have supremacy over the human heart.

My research clearly showed that Milton knew that many languages referenced courage as a word that meant keep heart, to care, to have passion, to long, to hope, to have within one's core—sensitivity, neediness, imagination, attachment, and love—and the passion to fully live these matters, no matter the cost. Milton knew the synonymous meaning of courage and heart, inextricable and, hence, unintelligible without the other. The Latin *cor* means heart; the French word for heart is *couer*, from which the English word courage is derived. The core in English is the center of one's being or the heart of someone. In German the word *kar*, or an initial shape of the word courage, refers to heart, and in Hebrew the word heart is *leb*, which refers to the center of one's being, the feelings out of which issue what matters to one's self. Out of these original words and their cultivated, original understanding, we derive the meaning of courage. Courage had always had its origins in care, hope, love, vulnerability, full-hearted participation in life, from which we derived passion, a willingness to be in pain for something or someone that matters more than the pain. We surrender to courage. We don't create it.

Included in the *Areopagitica*, a defense of free speech, Milton made a thinly veiled reference to Descartes' work being used to split the created self from creation; Milton knew full well that *cogito ergo sum*, "I think; therefore, I am," Descarte fashioned as a tool to validate *sentio ergo sum*, "I feel; therefore, I am"—not diminish it. But will, the will of man to escape his humanity, would eventually suppress the incipient substance of the human being, the diminishment of heart through the use of language and distortions of meaning. Milton had even written to Descartes, whom he had never met, to support him, even though the poet as prophet knew their words would eventually be overwhelmed. Though experimenting in good faith, Descartes would, rightly so, be considered one of the seminal thinkers in objectivity. Sadly, his work would be used to tell half of the story, and the human heart would be marginalized as of little consequence because of its mystery. The preeminence of the heart would be dethroned by the head of objectivity, rather than submissively be wedded to it.

Einstein had warned us of such about our pancognitive illusions and the fallacies that would follow if we made the intellect our god. "It has, of course, powerful muscles, but no personality. It cannot lead; it can only serve." He had also pointedly, with humor, stated that if you tell a fish it is to climb trees, it will spend its days doing that which it was not made to do, believing that it is defective, lacks will, and is a failure at life because it cannot climb trees. The misguided assumption would split the self from its moorings, creating insanity, or "unwholeness."

I stared into faces of an audience unmoved, disinterested, yet strangely rigid in their spectating. I saw them, while they looked at me. I remembered watching a Gila monster, still, instinctive only, without care, love, hate, no more than survival unto itself, and yet guarded marvelously by DNA to continue its life without recognition of doing so. It had no true thought because it had no true emotion; it functioned on pure brain stem, and its development from there was no more than a cliff.

I had created a new word to contrast how far creation, the word itself, had been taken from its original mooring and meaning. So as not to let what I had been watching happen for years now, words be twisted into signposts of misdirection, I brought "voidition" to the present. It means an act of seduction or drawing into the null or void. The action symbiotically and sycophantically works off of the foundations of creation and life force but makes nothing. It simply uses everything created to pull towards the black hole of not feeling and not knowing in its most basic form. Much like we thought of cancer before its cure.

No one noted the connection of the word I had introduced to how I saw it being proven in the group before me. I felt my own self slipping in a descent, a slide into discouragement, a settling into despair. Words continued to come out of my mouth uselessly, and yet I had no words within anymore. I was muted—a philologist without words doesn't exist. The antonym of "voidition"—creation—I suddenly saw as somehow silly, even childish.

My colleagues stared in still-face. I did not even exist; the words that left my mouth were bubbles floating for a moment, then popping. If I stepped any further into my attempts, the void waited for me. I looked upon the most decent of humans locked into a descent I had not fully realized until that very moment. I was to become one of them, even though I was hired to be the different voice, to keep the Collective honest, as were my five other colleagues. My investment, my work, my academic integrity, my desire, my being did not matter. If I breathed another wish to be accepted by them, I would lose what scraps of self I had left. With that gasping knowledge, I grasped a breath of truth and knew what I would do.

I had stood before these people, read seamlessly a paper fragmented to being unrecognizable, and no one made a move. After completing the final sentence, I looked up with the proper academic false humility, gathered my folder and watched as the expected applause began. Stepping off the dais, I moved to the right-hand side of the auditorium to head quickly down the aisle toward the back of the room. I was frightened.

I looked into a colleague's face, Dr. Sybil Williams, a notable and, most recently, highly praised member of a social science society. We had spoken numerous times when attending conferences. I looked into her face, a decent person, and saw nothing, not anything to register inner-self. Veiled eyes, unmistakably reptilian in presentation. She gave nothing back to me as I walked by and nodded to her in fear, knowing that I was nodding goodbye. She had already disappeared. I was frightened and very awake; as the fumes of despair swirled around my thoughts, sucking me down, my feet were guided by something else.

Looking into other faces as I moved toward the back of the room, I saw that everything had moved on. Patronized applause continued my first few steps down the aisle, and ended quickly. A panel member stood to gather the other panel members for summary discussion and comments about the papers, all of which were different, and of no consequence. The decisions had all been made before we arrived. We, the distinguished scholars, were tools of an agenda, hired by the Collective to be mavericks, to keep ideas alive so that dogma did not become death. We were hired in the name of representing trust in mystery and wonder. Instead we were public relations tools, pretending to be tension-keepers for honesty's sake, just things, collateral sacrifice of the best for all.

V

I loosened my tie as I walked the long distance to the back of the room, gathering some energy. I took the paper from my leather folder, a gift from the only woman in my life. She was a long way away, and I was awake to the distance. I dropped the paper in an empty chair, a paper that had brought together years of research, documentation, and travel. I then took off the tweed jacket that I had worn for years at every conference. We had purchased it in Scotland while doing postdoctoral and adjunct work at Edinburgh. The jacket had become my whiff of an attempt at vanity, as if it made me recognizable, my signature prop. I dropped it on top of the paper, opened the exit door quietly and escaped without a word, call, comment, or contact from that point onward. Never to return.

I did not know what I was going to do. I just knew I had to leave where I was and go home. I was without a plan, or purpose beyond home. But I was armed with a clear birth of a nebulous loss and passion formed in that room and forwarded to a hope in the memory of the future. Two days later I would begin to register the paragraphs. I would begin to hear what I would one day see.

When I walked into the night, away from the lights of the conference center, I could see the night sky. I looked up into the stars, found them alive and portending nothing of fate having any impact, much less a voice. Nor did I find the spaces between the lights of the stars of any consequence. The spaces were visual silence. Even so, a thought began to form in me like more useless noise. The silence visual allowed the sound of the visual to speak from me, not to me. Even after leaving the conference, knowing I had just ended my career, by choice, I continued my wondering, my thinking, at a time not fitting the occasion. My desire would not stop, nor the thoughts that came following them like ocean waves, languishing of roaring, they came, rhythmically mundane. I clenched a fist with nothing to hit. I couldn't even turn it off to have proper despair.

I stared at the stars, standing on a sidewalk, by myself, outside the Collective, and then I got it again. The spaces were visual silence that allowed the sound of the visual to speak from me. Symphonic visual experience, just as music uses silence to speak, giving the hearer opportunity to use the silence to speak from within, the breaks in the notes allow the response. The break in the stars allows response, the human factor to be in relationship with what is outside one's self.

Then I knew one truth, one very clear knowing within me. *Sentio ergo sum.* The link that connects everyone to everything and every other being who wishes to be connected. The human link to truth in a place of wonder, mystery and tragedy: *sentio ergo sum*. Milton refers to the hardening of the heart as the self-induced punishment of those who abuse the freedom of the will. Only humans can work against their predesign. No other creature except through abuse of will hides the heart of itself. Its "will" can only be submitted to its "desire" to live. We, the pinnacle of creativity, can be most asleep to how we are made, more asleep than a blade of grass. Writers, thinkers, philosophers, theologians, warriors, mothers, fathers, and children have spoken of such for centuries. The threads of truth about us remain ready to be woven by anyone who has a weaver's presence of art.

Without *sentio ergo sum* recognized in its certainties, just as certain as the organs of the body work for our good, no connection to our inner-selves can be made, and thus no connection of myself to others, between us, among us, or towards us can be made. We cannot even connect to the Creator; we aren't present. Descartes' attempt to find us whole proved to be more his undoing than ours. Even Lucretius who introduced us all to materialism and meaninglessness in *De Rerum Natura* did so only by willing away his own predesign. The will to stop the courage of the heart. The conflict was between the will to stop the heart and the submission of will to allow the heart's wonderings to be pursued. True submission, not subordination, is the mission of serving a greater mission than one's own individual power can sustain. A war of love began a long time ago, I saw, between entities that had become separated by refusal, one of which was to be submitted to the other.

I suddenly saw the conflicts that needed to be submitted for complementarity to produce multiplicity. The war of love for something, not against something. A yielding can produce a yield. A war of love, born in desire, carried by passion, lived in patience, continued by wisdom: light into darkness, creation into destruction, hope into despair, and courage into death. The will had been placed like an idol in the position of primacy. The rational had become the answer to the strife and struggle of living when it was to be only a tool of the heart for hopes to be fulfilled or grieved when lost.

We run from the demiurge within us, the craving for life that makes every child cry, rightly so; they see the limitations to their imaginations, their creation images, and thus, grieve. The tragedy in the tragedy is that we throw out the baby with the bath water. My goodness, I had slipped into the prosaic, the pacifying cliché. Now the word pacifying fits nicely with the baby reference, making the cliché functional. Perhaps I mistake obsession for creativity, and what I see as illumination is really childish wanderings. I mocked myself for what I could not stop and was made to do. I had not even seen what I taught.

I didn't have to care in that moment. The Collective wasn't assessing. I could be silly, like a child. I could cry like a child. I could feel despair like a child, who could not relinquish hope in the midst of the need to be cared for. Even despair had a reference point of hope. When children kept crying, humankind lived; without their tears, humankind just exists. The heart of kinship gets lost. The battle is for hearts; the war is for love. The indivisible had been rendered divisible by the illusion that had become delusion. The knowledge in me would become a skill, not a science. The old humanist in me would become the educated artistry of a person, not a humanist, post-anything, nihilist, functionalist, familiarist, or collectivist. And the man, well, the man would still have to be found.

This surrender made all the difference down to the cellular life movement of my very breath. I had found the universe again. It had been silenced by our deafness to our own hearts' voices that could hear through the silence. While finding the universe again, I had become mindless of where I was going on the ground. I laughed. I had walked at least a mile away from the conference center. I realized that I had been walking towards the airport. So what, so what, so what. Nothing useful. It was all over.

VI

As I walked in the starlight, the remorse, without bargain, began to settle inside me. I had been untrue to myself, to my people, to my family. We, active social philologists, had compromised to remain part of the Collective rather than face that no community could thrive when academia was subordinated to its own collective thought. I had been compromised in the abuse of the name of hope, and my own secret pleasure of egotistical aggrandizement. I had been permitted to be a "rebel." All six of us had gotten to see ourselves having identity separate from the Collective somehow, when we had actually been used to make the agenda seem forward looking. We were even being used to enable the Collective in its own denial. We were glossing over the loss of truth—real, livable, tangible, meaningful truth of life. Our sincerity, our "without wax" that exposes the sculptor's artistic imperfections, was used to hide their waxing over the eradication of meaning. Though I thought I perceived, I did not see; though I thought I heard, I did not listen. Had I seen and listened, I would have understood with my heart and maybe something else could have happened. I had such contempt for my ego, my own grandiosity; I had been a tool.

The silence of the night freed my heart to think, and the thick, warm air freed my body to be wrapped in sweat. My shirt was soaked from concentration and effort. I was at work. I had walked another mile before I suddenly remembered the etymology of the word obey—*obedire*—a Latin word that means to listen. The behavior that follows is only implied as a result of having listened to what matters to the listener. We cannot take in and value words that do not enhance our inner beings; we can fake or deny this reality, but we have to shut off our inner selves to do so. The Collective promises safety, not life. Obey means to listen. It does not mean, "Do what you are told to do" as a threat. Authority comes from the word author, one who wishes to be heard because they value their words and hope for others to benefit from them. An author gives words that they hope others will obey, listen to, and thus, behave. Behave does not mean do as one is told, either. It means to have being, or to become who you are. It implies taking action with the being one has at birth. And sacrifice does not mean giving something up; it means being able to participate in the sacred. Sacrifice is an opportunity, not a token action or demand. It is an invitation of participation. Passion moves it all; the willingness to be in pain for something that matters more than the pain. It does not destroy. It builds. The beauty of the word, obey, I had forgotten, and lost the wisdom that comes from its willingness. I took my cell phone out of my pants pocket and threw it as far as I could into the empty field beside me, and then unplugged my watch from my wrist with the Collective's receiver in it. I threw it as far as I could, too. I was awake; I was going home.

I tucked my tie in my shirt and ran from my brain, ran in hard-soled shoes along the deserted service road of what used to be New Orleans. I ran until my lungs hurt and my feet throbbed. When I finally stopped, worn out, I bent over for a while to breathe, my hands on my knees, soaking wet and loving the freedom of it all. I walked the rest of the way to the airport, sweaty and exhausted, almost peaceful. I caught the last flight out, picked up my car at midnight and drove the two hours home to our land, our forests, hills, and meadow.

I awakened after three hours sleep, slipped quietly out of the bed so as not to awaken Beatrice again; she slept soundly, having been up with me well into the early dawn hours. We would continue a long conversation when she awakened. She would not be at the hospital this morning. She had just finished her three-day rotation there working everywhere they needed her. Her work in the past in nursing in many of the places we had lived gave her experience in administration, crisis-management, surgical practices in primitive circumstances, and of course, working as a bed-side nurse. Before we met, she had already spent a year in Pujab, a year in the deserts near Dafir, and a year in Jellico Valley in the Appalachians. She had always been a caregiver, tough, compassionate, and yet had never become hardened to life. She didn't seem shocked by my appearance two days early, or by what I described. She had attempted to tell me as much along the way, but I couldn't hear. I had allowed myself to be deceived. I had fallen in the trap of believing in my own personal power and an area of ideals that denies that others will use a vision of goodness to control and destroy. So what. Stop thinking.

The sun blinked against the stone tiles in the hallway. Nothing was pressing but home, place, work; it could wait. I needed to wait. I hadn't been in this position since childhood. I made coffee, noticing the old name of Maxwell House with its new global logo. The coffee was the same, thankfully. Still good to the last drop. I stood at the window, watching the sun rise over our mountain, really just a great hill and ridge that ran along the whole east side of our place. It was covered with hardwoods towards the top along the ridge, cedars below, and hundreds of pines my sons and I planted years ago. In past years as they got older, we had cut out and laid out seven paths up the mountain. We had maintained them for years. My favorite was the steepest with a level section midway up that then turned into another steep flight to the top. From there, I could see all of our place and beyond, including the real mountain ranges in the distance.

I had not gone up the mountain in years; told myself the paths were for them anyway. They ran the paths until they left home. I used to love watching them jog the final flat space of the meadow. They always reminded me of horses cantering in tandem, headed towards the barn at the end of the day.

I put down my empty cup, a mug my youngest son had made. He made the whole set of our daily serving dishes. I took a deep drink of cold water and headed to our mud porch that exited to the outside. Putting on running boots, a sleeveless topper over my shirt, and some old running pants, I planned to go to the top of the mountain, if I could get there. I had not breathed deeply in a long time, unless I counted last night. My work had become the majority of my life, even my worth. Bea and I no longer even travelled together, no more working in the same territories of interest; she had been offered much by the Collective, but decided to help where we lived.

I headed up seven. I ran slowly through the meadow, still able to see the path that grass had taken back over since there had been no footsteps in over three years. I could see dew on the grass and light glinting off early morning spiders' webs stretched between daisy stems and broom sedge stalks. I caught a rhythmic breath, ever grateful to be home, my body remembering the old habits of these lands as I made the 1.5 mile climb to the top of the ridge. The stones we had set to get across the wet weather draw were still in place; so too were the 50 yard, or 46.4 meter, section of level ground we had created of dirt, rock, and log supports on the sides. That summer project they got me to join in on. It cut across a ravine and could hold water on the uphill side when we had a lot of rain. Wildlife used it. Tracks of raccoons and deer were easily recognizable in the soft ground near the water.

At the top, my legs burned and truthfully, I barely made it, but the joy of being here made the ache worth it. I caught my breath, leaning against a red oak tree, and then looked out over our small meadow, the ball field backstop, and then the dry stack rock wall that ran more than a quarter mile along the edge of the meadow. Two old men from the mountains north and I had built the wall when the boys were little. I could see lilies blooming brightly from this distance. The yellow blooms reached toward the east sunrise and stretched along at least half of the wall. Some wide steps of stone led up out of the meadow towards the outbuildings, garden, and then the home with windows all across the back, always uncovered to catch a sunrise or rising storm. We had shared many a meal looking out over that meadow and ridge.

Sometimes the four of us sat on the same side of the long table to watch a storm. Bea said the storm was our guest today. I remember looking down the table to say something to someone at the other end as if at a diner counter. I always smiled at the scene. Our sons grew up on this place from ages five and seven. We raised them to manhood here. The oldest lived farther north; the youngest farther south. They had pitched the Collective's receivers before they left home. I thought they showed immaturity; "energy without vision," I called it. They actually evidenced how they were raised in spite of my blind illusions; they saw before I saw. They all saw before I saw.

I looked down at the top of my left wrist, noting the small black cap covering the jack that the receiver in my watch had linked to. Anyone without a receiver remained separated from communication except for handwritten mail and face-to-face talk. I had thrust myself back to a time before wireless communication and even the old landline connections. Even the men from the north mountains did not remember a time before wireless. And wireless was slowly being replaced by optic-laser cybernetics. I had heard that some special reserved places were already using laser guided material transport that reorganizes molecular structure, actually sending objects to other locations in milliseconds. No animate object had been transported based upon my cursory research. The satellites of the past were still being used in the same air space, but they were outfitted with laser technology that bypassed wave technology and, therefore, atmospheric restraints. Operational laser "zero-space" cybernetics had improved geographical communication and speed beyond what I had believed possible. All the landline connections were gone, taken over years ago by a very rational approach to linkages. I knew the history and completely supported the efficiency of those historical decisions.

Now I clearly saw where they led us. Even the delivery of mail had become sporadic in its dependability. The need for competent folks had receded and there was little support from the Collective to keep it going. While I had not gone to my own mailbox in years, Bea had been using it for some time now. Letters from both my sons would arrive and we would read them like archaeological discoveries, going over them with a soft brush, reading between the lines to conjure up understanding. They were involved in some things they lightly referenced but did not speak about specifically. Bea and I could only trust. We knew their characters and the integrity of their hearts.

I remembered a quote from an author named Steinbeck, from the mid-twentieth century; it was from a book called *East of Eden*. A character says of a power craver, "Some men can't see the color green, but they may never know they can't. I think you are only a part of a human.... I wonder whether you ever feel that something invisible is all around you. It would be horrible if you knew it was there and couldn't see or feel it. That would be horrible."

Remorse suddenly flooded me even in the midst of gratitude, maybe because of it. I was awake and knew again the burdensome pain of love.

I remembered their seriousness and play, their work with me and our times together, all of us. I remembered Beatrice's smile and the lightness of her laughter, not having heard it from her in years. I had become less than myself. I had distanced myself from the substance of what matters to the human heart, my own, me, from what mattered more. I had lost my way, gotten off familiar mountain paths. Everything grew quiet but my breathing and the beat of my own pulse. My sides tightened and then the exhale told the whole truth of what was missing. I slid down the trunk of the red oak, and quietly wept.

I had been gone a long, long time. I had not seen, and thought others were blind. Now the blind man could see and through my tears I could see my future right in front of me.

I wanted to live life again. Whatever I needed to do, I would offer. I did not know exactly what the change would look like, where I was to take this decision I had made the night before, but I did know that I would not return to the Collective. Last night already seemed like a long time ago. I rose after the sun had begun to warm the day and headed home.

VII

O n the way down the trail home I did some chin ups on low hanging limbs. I also pulled my body up a few tree limbs using only arms, feet used only to stabilize. I used to be able to pull up quite a ways into the trees before needing to use my feet to push. That ability had rescinded from lack of use. Still, it felt good to sweat, to be alive, even though I could feel the weariness in my deeper regions. My muscles were still flexible and able though underused. I walked back slowly, taking time to observe what I had missed, and to let the rest begin to sink in.

When I got to the back porch entrance, Beatrice called to me from our courtyard. She had arisen and sat in the calm morning warmth until I returned. She had seen me coming through the meadow toward her and our home and watched the sun shining on the grass and the old ball field backstop. A gas water and coffee awaited me. She drank hot tea. I had been drinking gas water for years. We had discovered them in Italy, Tuscany actually, Bea's favorite place on earth, besides Trunk Bay in St. John's.

I told her more about the night before after we had sat

quietly for some time. She looked to the distances above the hills as I talked. Her eyes were concentrated, kind, and full of thought as she looked back to me. After I finished the story about walking out of the conference, she just said, "good" and then smiled, her eyes crinkling at the edges. I wondered what she knew. Then, she said very simply, staring straight into me. "It's time for all of us to reach without compromise, and time for you to grow up."

I looked at her confused and sheepishly, smirking a bit. I had seen the first comment coming, but not the second, though somehow I intuited that she had something to give me. Her words did not have insult attached to them. I had an awareness, a rustling inside me, felt it on the mountain like hearing my name in the wind of the oak leaves still hanging on before spring leaves push them away. Her words called to me, not to my credits. I had been quite the adult in my profession. Before I could even think about claiming my place with more words, she went on to tell me about her desire to have the rest of me, she described as the heart I left behind as I became more and more convinced that powers of persuasion could change someone, or even an institution.

For the next 42 days straight I ran the mountain paths harder and harder, listening at the top each time, working my body out in the trees on the way down. I began to feel strong again, and my shoulders, arms, and hands returned to their former strengths, though age had slowed my full endurance. I felt strong and rested, yet without direction for the passion that moved inside me. Bea and I talked, did chores, worked in our garden as spring rolled towards summer. We walked long distances over the region, its woods, meadows and hills. We picnicked in the shade of giant ash and pine trees up on the trails, talked long about our pasts, our sons, dreams, regrets, travels, celebrations and losses to grieve; and we talked much about our willingness to surrender to whatever the future brought to us rather than give ourselves to the Collective. We read letters from our sons that spoke of rumblings in other regions in the north sections and the south sections. They spoke of their love for us, too, and I was thrilled with being a part of such connection. I had been removed for longer than I knew. Beatrice smiled more, shared more.

I noticed that I started looking at sections of books in the evenings and early mornings before the sun rose. Great books and minor works, plays, histories, fiction, poetry, descriptions of art. I noticed that paragraphs settled into my mind like storage of food, and plans for dinners when the food would be used for communion. The absorption of paragraphs like veins of gold that reached in tendrils to the mother lode sank into me. I began to feel the gravitas of words; their messages and the heartbeat in them that let the people who wrote them live, though their bones had already returned to dirt.

I had known words, but had not taken in the heart of the authority from which they came. I had always tried to cram more and more into my insatiable and gifted brain, blind to how I never fed my own heart.

The paragraphs that absorbed into me were heart messages from people who could not live, lest they spoke what they could not keep silent. Author gave words to a listener, a reader, to give them life. The author gave his heart if they were true, and the listener gave obedience if the author sought the good of the one who sought more for his life. Only those words that spoke that love could I absorb and keep. All other words dropped to the ground at my feet, shards of useless clay pieces, good for the gravel pile. Nothing wasted. The words that became cellular confirmed a way of thought, a way of being, a way of the heart. My crazy thoughts on the service road the night I left were gold thoughts coming from true places, not shards. To deny the words meant not having one's life.

I recalled Gabriel Marcel's words; though I could not remember their source, I remember sitting on the banks of a stream where I had gone to fish, but instead sat and read in the sunlight while the stream glided past. I could see the words broken by memory yet true. "Existence is inseparable from a certain astonishment.... . Personally, I am inclined to deny that any work is philosophical if we cannot discern in it what may be called the string of reality... . It may be said in this respect that no concrete philosophy is possible without a constantly renewed tension between those depths of our being in and by which we are; nor without the most stringent and rigorous reflection, directed on our most intensely lived experience..."

Those words signified much of the other words of paragraphs that stuck to my ribs. If they did not speak to my being of heart and speak to my good, even to the neglect of safety, I found the words empty and the author twice so because they sought control rather than my best. They themselves were hiding their emptiness and wanted to use me to help them. The gold string of creation and the deep-based backbeat hum of creating, all the true authors had in common. They spoke with one voice in the multiplicity of creation about one thing. Living with courage to live fully; loving deeply in that courage; leading well in heart so that something of value is left behind. They all knew; they all strove for it.

VIII

———

I had been thinking such thoughts on the top of one of the trails. I watched the sun set and listened to the wind in the trees. The day had been warm and rich. I could see storm clouds forming off in the distance, lightning strikes so far away no sound came in the thunder. I didn't realize how late it had gotten, how darkness had already arrived, and the crickets and other evening bugs had begun their soft scratching calls. I had become very comfortable on the paths, but not ready to do them blind. Walking back down in the dark, I did not realize that I had stepped off the path of trail six. I stumbled a bit and tried to go slower, frustrated by my internal wanderings that left me in the dark; my frustration moved me to hurry. I became unusually confused about my exact location and could see no lights from home.

I then tripped on the thick, gnarly roots of a maple, able to feel the bark to know the tree, and fell hard and fast. Instead of hitting firm ground, I kept falling like through a trap door that had been covered with leaves and twigs. Landing hard with a thud, a loud grunt of air came out of me. I had to have fallen eight to ten feet. The ground was soft and pliable in my hands as I tried to push up; I was scared and unable yet to breathe. My left shoulder took the blow and my side hurt. Before I could get my bearings, I heard another breath and smelled a stench of rot and sewage; something tore with slicing power into my boot all the way to my ankle.

I pulled away quickly in searing pain as a whip type sound of something under my left eye suddenly cut into my cheek, barely missing my eye and the rest of my face as I pulled backwards instinctively in terror, not even registering the sheer pain. I heard the muffled sound of a heavy weight land against the dirt wall above my head. Thrashing about like a drowning man, I pushed up towards the place I thought I had come from. My right hand landed on a root above my shoulder and I pulled towards it, dragging myself against the wall of wherever I was, kicking my feet wildly, as furiously as I could, pulling to find other roots to pull me up to the surface. My feet landed several blows with dull cracking sounds and yet a dull sinking into the creatures. I swung once to free myself, as my left shoulder, along the base of my neck down my arm, was ripped downwards not by a pull but by a slicing open of my flesh. I heard grunting, a deep garbled growl, and the heat and stench of breath on my face.

With little time left, I knew death was coming. I kept pushing, grabbing roots, pulling with what might I had, desperately trying to get home. I growled and screamed, pushing upwards, my feet kicking against the body surfaces of the creatures as I went up. They were becoming ground to push against. I kept landing blows with my boots, hard as I could deliver while pushing upwards. Bea wouldn't know what happened to me. Grunting and muffled snarls were the only audible sounds, hard scaled and mushy at landing kicks with my boots and my cries at the pain of the cut down my lower back, my left foot pushing off a head or a shoulder to bring me to the surface of the earth and the darkness I could finally see.

I rolled over and over, trying to move away and downward to home, away from whatever had just happened. I was alone, for a last breath, waiting to die. I breathed hard, flat on my back, staring straight through the leaves into a three-quarter moon, and the sounds of the night were just like they had been only minutes ago. Whatever they were didn't follow me above ground. I wondered for a second if I was dreaming. The blood and the pain left no illusion that the night would ever be normal again. As confused as I was, I knew the way home. Just move downhill. Find the light and move toward it like a ship to the lighthouse. I stood slowly, leaned ever so briefly against a nearby sapling almost dropping to the ground again against its slim bending give. I unsteadily let my body weight move me downward, knowing I had to make it, knowing I would get home to see Bea if nothing else, very alive, very alive. I found the light, relieved to have the direction and stumbled forward with one thought.

My weight rested all to my right. My left ankle was twisted and bleeding. My left shoulder was operable. I could not tell anything about my back, but I had felt the cutting start below my shoulder blade ripping down to my lower spine. I pushed up the back steps, calling in short gasps for Beatrice. She came quickly and looked as scared as I must have been. Not even asking what happened, she went straight to work, grabbing scissors and cutting my bloody clothes off after I collapsed gratefully into a wooden chair on our back porch. I stared at her face; she was focused on saving her patient. I then looked into the lights on the porch, and rested in spite of the pain. Blood was all over me, and I was home.

She wrapped a sheet around me, telling me about the wounds, her sense of what was needed, as she got the truck keys to get to the emergency room. She said the cuttings were in groups of four slices, clearly evident as we went out the front of the house. She helped me slowly into the truck; I had to slump sideways because of the wounds down my back. The wounds looked like scalpel or razor cuts, each about an inch deep. As we sped down the highway, she glanced at my face that was already drowsily looking towards her. The cut just below my left eye, she noted, obviously missed, because only one slice-mark had landed. She and I both knew that had the blow landed in my neck or more about my head, the weight of the creatures and the cuttings would have finished me, and left her without me again.

We sped down the two-lane highway, the trees along our path a blur to me as each of us settled into the lull of a spellbound pain and silence, Bea glancing over at me to check on me, worry and compassion in her eyes. I reached out to her with my right hand and told her that I believe I had discovered my next step in life, trying to smile a little. Beatrice just said, "You are ridiculous," and shook her head smiling, too, amidst this insanity. Years were in our past. They only brought us closer to each other.

I now understood what our sons had been talking about. I thought they had dropped somehow into wild hyperbole or phantasms of a sort, maybe even code language. They had been speaking literally about reality and the truth into it. Metaphor and truth, reality and the concrete had merged finally and the war of love that I had thought about on the road from the conference to the airport was not poetic wanderings, but real, living, breathing reality. I said to Bea quietly, "For those with eyes" our sons had both written, "we move light into darkness, hope into despair, creativity into destruction, and courage into the face of death." They had also used an old quote from the New Testament that said, "Though seeing, they do not see; though hearing, they do not hear or understand." I quit talking for a moment and remembered the rest that I spoke clearly to her:

"The people's heart has become calloused; they hardly hear with their ears and they have closed their eyes. Otherwise they might see with their eyes, hear with their ears, understand with their hearts and turn, and I would heal them."

Even in the midst of my body beginning to awaken from shock and with the pain beginning to overwhelm me,

I was even more overwhelmed by what hit me. I turned my face to the deserted highway, the headlights pushing into the night, and said, "I was mauled almost to death by swallowed selves; the self is imprisoned in the creature. It then feeds off of the created's energy system, sucks out of its heart, the core place those truth tellers have always spoken about." Our sons were living the metaphor, the breathing metalanguage of the hard truth that is reality. It had come. The symbol was the truth; the metaphor the reality. It breathed and almost killed me. I felt pain in my heart and foolish for not seeing what my sons had known for some time.

"Have you known?" I asked Bea as we pulled in close to the emergency entrance. She glanced over to me as she put the truck in park, very focused as a nurse, and spoke quickly before getting out to help me, "I sensed something, but didn't know for sure until tonight. Too many of us were disappearing and it seemed to fit with what the letters were saying." She then got out quickly and came around to my side of the truck, opened the door and began to help me out; stiffness was making it hard for me to move. I put my right arm around her shoulder, and we limped in. "From what I gather from tonight and the letters," she said to me as the doors slid open and attendants began to move towards us, seeing that this was not a normal walk-in emergency, "everyone who rescues has a region to create in, to create a refuge and rescue station. That is all I have been able to decipher. The letters indicate as much without saying specifically."

"But, Abe," Bea leaned close to my face and looked straight into my eyes just as I was lowered into a wheelchair, the blood from the sheet getting all over it, "we, all of us, are in trouble. Somehow, our time has come." I saw in her face before we headed back into the rooms just how much she loved me beyond this night of pain, and what she meant, finally, by my growing up. I remembered something from one of the paragraphs as I was placed gently on my right side on the examining table, now very weak from loss of blood and the bizarre nature of how life operated. I couldn't place it, then realized dimly that the doctor who had just walked in had said, "Life has scars who live it," as he leaned over me to look at my face. He told me very softly in a kind voice that I would be fine, but that I would have to "hurt more before so." I had not heard that ancient reference to time in years, realizing as I slid into a twilight unconsciousness with the fluids and sedatives dripping into me, that the old phrase was Scottish.

I came to some hour and a half later, Bea standing nearby as the attendant offered me sips of charged water and ice. I immediately recognized the doctor's voice as he stepped into the curtained area. He moved towards me with a soft smile. He wore a bowtie, crisp white shirt and jacket. His graying bushy eyebrows and mustache only highlighted his crystal blue eyes, startling to me even in my condition. Placing a hand on my shoulder, no questions about my condition, he began to tell me about another case, of a man he had known for some "seasons," a 2nd generation Scotch-man who "lived over the mountain and a league or so from hence." The fellow had received several more body wounds and escaped similarly.

His hand communicated gentleness, care, firmness, yet his words were detached from his care. He spoke with some urgency, the verbal message being important enough to override any questions about my wounds. He had already informed me that they would heal. I assumed he expected me to simply believe it. I didn't challenge him; somehow I had no need.

He then said, "I am consterned about you." I looked straight into his eyes as he spoke, catching the Middle English word, derived from French, founded in Latin. He was telling me that he himself carried within him consternation, a care for me versus having a passing thought or passing experience of me as part of his vocation only. The word expressed the difference between ownership and leasing. This unusual Scottish physician clearly knew of my background as a philologist, and was communicating with me on many levels. Then, he added, "clare constat," an ancient Scottish legal term that means, "it is clearly established." I could only discern in my condition that he spoke of a care for me that had in it a kinship and an expectation. He trusted me to gather his words and understand. He expected me to grasp with a steely mind and a committed heart that I mattered to him way beyond my physical condition. He obviously trusted my mind and heart more than I did at the moment, and he expected my wounds to be secondary.

He looked at me and then at Bea in the face, nodded as if I gathered all that was happening, squeezed my knee gently as he turned to leave the recovery room. He said he would come to our home to check on me tomorrow afternoon.

"You will be sore, for sure. Now be thankful that you have such an extraordinary woman beside you." His last words were "good den," Old English, which meant that the goodbye was only temporary like a parent speaks to a child with, "rest well and I'll see you in the morning."

Bea and I walked slowly to the truck. I thanked this "extraordinary woman" as she buckled my seatbelt for me. Reaching to her face with my free hand, I stalled her movements for a minute. She teared and hugged me gently. I stroked her hair for a moment. We both knew that this night was the beginning of sorts and that we were in it together no matter what the cost. We drove home without much comment, deeply in thought, but in the same place with them. We knew that something had command of the dark, and that our days had become illusions of a normal that was gone.

IX

B ea pulled onto the river gravel drive after midnight. She helped me take off the old work jacket I kept in the truck as we came in the front foyer. Everything looked the same, the soapstone dark gray tile, the cross beam timbers, the windows, now darkened that looked out on to our meadow and hills. But everything had changed again. Beatrice carried the slashed topper and t-shirt in a bag. Four razor-like slashes, slicing claw cuts like scalpels left her wondering even as exhausted as we were. I was numb from the tiredness and the wonders of medicine to dull pain, though my mind still turned as did hers.

After she turned to shut the door, she looked up and reached gently to my left eye, saying, "I'm so sorry; it's swelling more." After looking into her concern, I glanced into the mirror on the wall by the door to see my reflection. After looking at my eye, and how bedraggled and swollen the left side of my face was, I noticed how good her short ponytail looked with her hair pulled back. I would never be able to stop seeing her, no matter what my condition. That sometimes was like medicine to be able to extend past myself, and painful because I could. Even now.

I took off the hospital gown as I limped into our den, and threw it away in the kitchen. Standing there in my underwear, I offered Bea a crooked smile and offered to help make omelets. "I stir with my right arm; you cook. How 'bout it?" She walked out of our back porch mudroom and pulled an old flannel button up over my shoulders, and put slip-on shoes on my feet. My deal to help stir didn't work out well. After pushing a button for quiet music, I sat and really didn't have energy to move much more. *Vox Silentii* played quietly over the speakers as Bea moved about making toast, omelets and coffee.

We sat quietly with the soft music surrounding us as we ate and drank coffee into early morning. When she rose to take the dishes, I did too, catching her just in time to take her hand and pull her to me. Holding her with my right arm, we held each other gently. We washed dishes. She said softly, "I'm not afraid; our sons are not afraid; our fear has turned into daily faith. My daily fear is now my need to risk wisely and trust deeply in the serenity that comes from knowing our place. My anger is a willingness to follow how we are made. I'm all in Abe." She looked to my eyes searchingly. I thought of Buber's report of the Hasidic parable. The Creator does not ask Rasmov how good he was at being Moses; Creator asks him how good he was at being Rasmov. She loved me completely, beyond what I had stepped into.

Then, she said, "The Collective does not seek liberty in

these matters. You know it. Had you not come to this place today physically and mentally, you would be dead. Had you been on the mountain where you were just a short time ago, you would be dead." She touched my forearm and then my cheek. "You would be gone forever," her voice catching as tears slid down her cheeks. "The Collective wants peacekeepers, not peacemakers. I love you Abe, with all I have in me."

"I love you," I said, turning my head like a golden retriever attempting to grasp the meaning of a voice. I reached out with my right hand and brushed her tears away. "Let me help you get ready for bed," she said tiredly. "You will be sore tomorrow, and tomorrow, we sit. I will take care of you. Do you understand?" The nurse had taken over. "You sit; rest; I will take care of you. Got it?" I nodded in assent as we headed for the bedroom. "Got it," I said.

Beatrice settled me in on my side, stitches down my back and down my left shoulder made being on my back or stomach too painful. As she lay down beside me, she said that we need much prayer. She said that she believed that the whole earth groaned for its return. I recognized the reference in the ancient book of Romans, nature itself, along with us in it, groaning to return to what it is made to be. I heard again the words from the night I left the conference: *Sentio ergo sum.* Anaurosis had ended; my own had come to sight. I floated some on those thoughts, jumbled and moveable. She put her fingers through my hair. I asked, "What is going on?" The pills and weariness in my bones dragging me down into a falling sleep. Beatrice sat up with her back against the headboard as I dropped into sleep. I felt her body slide down next to mine gently after she knew that she could now rest, too.

Then came the dream, the dream in its archetypal imagery, its symbols in myth and mystery, unfinished business of defenses and identification in the literary movements of our history. My deciphering was no help to me this time. This dream was not an object. The sight exposed me to the rest of myself and the life of truth I was made to live. I was being, not just seeing. No more half-life or waiting for life. The gravity of gravitas was coming my way.

X

—————

I remember exactly what occurred, slowly and painfully, deeply humiliated to be exposed as thinking that I could avoid creation. That I could live fully as an impostor in my own skin, and not be found out if I really wanted to live what I said I believed.

I stood in the middle of a golf course fairway. I had followed my slice off of the tee box and was close to my second shot. I was alone. I looked up and an empty golf cart whipped by me bumping and bouncing along the ground in the middle of the fairway, behind which a polar bear came roaring along lumbering at top speed. It was running from something I could sense by its face the way its ears laid back. A low flying chicken flew along just above the polar bear, going as fast as it could, with the speed of a hawk, all in front of a horse and rider moving as one. The horse's ears pointed forward and nostrils flared; the rider sat upon the horse, a steely, sinewed man, a close cropped grayish beard, hat pulled down on his head, not quite like a cowboy hat but without show, usable and well-worn. He wore a sun-bleached blue shirt; face set fiercely and with a joy more than a smile. He rounded a rifle with one arm, a Winchester 73 of the ancient west, dead aim on a path towards the polar bear.

The golf course, which I did not suit, and the horse and rider, which I did not grasp, disappeared. I was no longer on a fairway; I was on the path of the rider's impact and presence somehow.

I then stood before a polar bear, stuffed and standing on a wooden platform; at its full height, paws to face, it stood 12 feet, claws and arms extended, frozen in a ferocious dead stare of jaws wide open to stop any threat. I remember a numb fear, even knowing a taxidermist had finished the bear. Even dead, I was reminded of my limits. The hunter had made this catch and moved on. What seemed like wanton power frightened me more than the bear. The bear had run from the hunter, frightened, when alive.

Then, the scene moved to a hallway on the left hand side of a shotgun house. The outer wall was to my left so that the rooms were like displays I walked by. I passed by a room as I walked towards the back of the house, an old house like in the photos of circa 1930s. The room was completely open, no wall between hallway and room. The double bed, a bow bed, nightstand, and a cane bottom, ladder-back chair were the only furnishings. I looked in the bed in time to see my father. He barely noticed me with glazed eyes, then pulled the sheet over his shoulders and head, covering him like a shroud while lying on his side with his knees pulled up in a fetal position.

I moved on without choice, pulled towards a place. I walked into a bathroom, white tile with small black diamonds uniformly highlighting the patterns that spread and repeated, spread and repeated. I entered through a white door, with three horizontal panels and a brown painted metal doorknob. I passed a small linen closet on the right side before the room opened up larger. My focus intensified as I gathered in the scene in a well-lighted room, with a sink, commode and chair.

The hunter stood by the far wall six feet across, six feet away, leaning without discomfort against the wall with his arms folded. The woman I knew; the woman I married sat on the commode. She wore a purple blouse that draped just below her waist. The purple I knew to be an old dye of shellfish, thousands of shellfish to create a purple of such royal, such rich yet worn color. Unbuttoned from neck to pelvis, her body revealed a warmth and lushness of fulfillment, willingness, comfort and dignity. From the depth of her eyes, to the curve of her neck to the hair between her thighs radiated full womanhood bordered by royalty. Her toes pointed against the ground like a ballerina's pose, presenting her in perfect symmetry and wholeness, completed and certain.

She had made love to the man, and she was without doubt, his, through and through. I looked at her with wounded dismay, and then gathered myself as I moved hard towards the hunter, grabbed his left forearm and realized that a boy, a sniveling one had grabbed a man. He did not sneer, but rather looked at me with pity, more as a curiosity, as if he now knew something about me. He moved away from the wall and out of the room slowly, neither of them looking at each other. The woman, once my wife, waited to be taken while she remained sitting, human necessity and divinity where I saw her. He left. She looked towards me more with curiosity than criticism and said, "What did you expect?"

I fell to the ground weeping with my head on my curled arm that hid my face. My arm and face rested on the seat of a metal chair, and my lower body was folded together at my side the way a girl sits in a skirt. I looked under the seat at a pool of tears that were my own urine. A perfectly formed pool of self-pity, crocodile pain, and loss that wouldn't work as true grief. My tears were piss and her urine was dignity.

Her words struck me and I knew what I had hidden from. I rose, facing my destiny, knowing what made the man look at me with such curiosity, like a mood had been released or a memory of someone that did not exist except as a dream dimly lit and of no consequence. The world died in me that moment. A reformation rose from the look, and the man who left stood up, looked at the woman; she rose from her repose, took two steps and slid into the arms of the hunter who had finally come. She gave herself to him. And the dream stopped forever.

I came to the next day, slowly awakening not far from daybreak. In the depths of creation where gold is streaked through harsh ore and diamonds pressured into clarity from blackness, I had come to me. Looking to my right from my back, which I had slept on without pain, lay the woman in the dream. I saw the one who had wanted for me to claim my place, and would never have fully known what she had missed until I did.

From that day onward I hunted from the inside out to find those createds who had been trapped by the outside creatures. I didn't understand much yet, but I knew that my mind had settled and my heart had risen. I never hunted for sport as the other one had in the dream. I hunted for life. He needed a memory of mercy. I needed to see the unseen creation and move as creation moves.

XI

———

The Scottish physician came to visit me, ostensibly to check my dressing and wound, which Beatrice could easily have done, being highly experienced in treating wounds and, sad to say, many infections that led to unnecessary deaths because the medicine and the educated attention were not in time. The Collective was going to attend to these worldly problems, but instead the death tolls had risen after food supplies did not meet demands; sickness increased, infection increased, violence increased, grief increased, numbness increased.

Although I was sore as expected, I was grateful to be alive and felt inside me a firmness, a sense of fixedness, which isn't even a word, but suddenly it wasn't about being right anymore. The word true mattered more than right.

The doctor opened his black satchel, one that had to be an antique to say the least. The MD medicine bag had disappeared when we got organized, when doctors became institutionalized, and medicine edged into business, and business became government. He wore the same bowtie, a fresh starched white shirt and vest that fit the spring weather. His eyes smiled but his face did not this day. His jaws carried such seriousness that seemed to have nothing to do with my injuries, but with a preoccupation. Yet his eyes spoke expectancy, even a laugh of a sort, in the depths and the corners. From that day onward, this man was simply known as "Doctor." His name suited who he had become.

He saw me glance into his bag and see an unusual instrument for such a visit. A dagger, unique in shape because of its seemingly perfect symmetry. It rested in a metal sheath; on the sheath were symbols and markings from seven powerful historical cultures. The markings could only be recognized by someone educated to know them because teaching of history had been left largely a blank since the changeover. History now started with the story of the enlightenment of Collective wisdom. Though he noted my curiosity, he began to hum while he checked my wounds. The humming, I noted, was a ballad of Scottish liberty. It was old, very old, yet I recalled it from my studies there, now what seemed a lifetime ago. The ballad's words spoke of broken hearts mended and warriors restoring the land to make a refuge for those who shaped it and for searchers, both.

Clearing his throat as he stopped the examination and the humming, he stated that the appearance of healing was on course rightly, but they would heal very slowly. An infection of poison that caused the patient to become dazed and eventually aggressive had been noted in other cases like mine. Strangely, he said, that the folks who had become infected possessed a certain character that had indicated some significant toxicity before they had fallen into an attack. He believed that I would heal inside and out. He also stated that he had seen and studied these cases in numerous geographical regions, which made my head tilt towards him with sharp interest and confirmation of my own intuition.

"Well now," he said as he looked straight into my eyes with stony seriousness, "seems to me, we need to get to what matters." Then, he began to recite a poem.

> *Your scars are your stories of a time deeply hoary,*
> *Of blackness coming to be pierced,*
> *While warriors wild move to be knighted.*
> *Courage they cried before dawn made dusk.*
> *We ride to rid lost souls of their husks.*
> *We ride 'til the sunset bleeds past death.*
> *We ride to the scent of clover on the wind's breath.*
> *No day, no night, but hope aloud,*
> *Until we come together finally with heads bowed.*
> *Hearts enlivened not death to see,*
> *Together we quest on the depths of the seas.*

I quickly became irritated by his seriousness becoming another something I had to grasp instead of him telling me straight, until I became startled to realize what he referenced. He looked at me and said, "You have a good memory, dear sir," as I stared at him. I did remember. The lines were from a Celtic prophetic prayer discovered on the wall of a monastery cell, circa 14th century. Very unusual to have carvings in the cells, and yet the oddity of it removed it from fitting into a total picture of the times and its contextual significance. Some scholarly monographs had been written about the lines, but for the most part they simply remained an archaeological find, cataloged and filed. I had noted it to memory for no particular reason except that of late I could see how it merged into the paragraphs that I could not help but search for, return to and feed my heart the food of them. All of these movements were so much of a whispered roaring backbeat to the numinous of life that I could not grasp anything at the moment, like drifting in a cascade or drowning in air, and yet I was a part of it all.

"That is what you are to do," Doctor said. "The memory of those words matter more than your actions. But without your actions, the words will never live for you or for the ones you pursue.

"Now is the time. I will send you a letter to explain everything we know at this time, including explanations of words that will not have much substance yet, like 'transporters' and 'restoration procedures.' However, suffice it to say, you have truly met your enemy. It is darkness, destruction, despair, and death. You are to 'save the children's lives,' so to speak. You are not alone. The American Coast Guard's military purposes were unlike other services. The purpose was to rescue, to save lives, so it patrolled and pursued, advocating its energies to fight for the ones in need." After giving me the dagger, he left with a severe nod and a hand laid gently on my right shoulder, and he did the same with Beatrice as he stood to leave.

The letter, really an epistle and operations manual combined, explained everything that we would need to know, except the toll on us emotionally and spiritually. It assumed the burden and assumed the responsibility of us to replenish well in the midst of the living. It also stated questions that would arise as we proceeded, and stated that they would be answered as discoveries were made. It simply reminded us that we were not alone in this quest.

The information clearly showed us that much work had preceded our specific involvement, quite a few years, in fact. We learned about times to hunt, behaviors of the creatures, cutting and "birthing" rescue techniques, cleansing methods, numbers, and transport schedules for pick-up and transfer methods. We were the epicenter for our region, which was basically as far as I could run between darkness and dawn.

The phosphorescence was a neuro-chemical-spiritual substance siphoned off the life-light within the createds. The creatures fed off of the heart energy of one's true being. Each of the createds had bargained with their lives unwittingly and yet knowingly. They all had attempted to find some way around life, to have safety from having to experience it as we are made. The explanation in science of the bio-neuro-physiological changes that actually swallowed a person's identity within the sheath of a poisonous and grotesque creature, we did not grasp yet. But we did see that somehow the emotional and spiritual had moved way beyond axiomatic effects upon attitude and physical wellbeing. The inner world had become transmuted into the outer results, results that no one would have sought in the bargain to have safety. Acute misery and cursed isolation of survival had taken over the wish to find a way out of pain.

The dagger—a 6 ⅞ inch blade and the same length handle, with a quarter inch guard to protect my hand from its double razor sides was exactly 14 inches from blade tip to handle end. Perfectly balanced and sacredly designed, it fit into my hand organically. My heart, my mind, my hands, and the blade worked as a passion with a purpose in a plan.

I trained on the mountain, we read and we ate well, planted and grew food, fed and rescued, lived on small royalties, dwindling savings from our former life, planned to be used for other things now long forgotten, and a consistent deposit in our account from an anonymous giver. And we hunted and recreated.

The hunting took me farther from home in the region that mattered to me, where I belonged. Up earlier to go out, running farther home. Seven years we had found them. Seven years of deep fulfillment. The paragraphs carried my heart on many a black night. They all spoke of the same deep primogenial heart of us longing for our home and the verities that remain changeless.

The multiplicity of ways that we attempt to split away from the heart of ourselves are countless, and yet the sentence of Gibran still rang true in reference to how we are created: "they are life's yearning for itself." I felt it, lived in it, breathed it and wanted the createds to have it back.

The nights' hunts took me out to the farthest edge of the region, beyond which I could not make a rescue and be at the tank in time to regenerate the life of the created, even though life before death beat the misery of dying as a part of the creatures viscera when it had drained the heart completely. I hunted in concentric outgoings until the region became essentially clean. The trees' leaves told the story of the root systems being vibrant again instead of cut up and bled out of their ability to absorb light and store energy in their roots. What we had years ago considered to be a blight related to the environment was actually creatures scarring and feeding. All the leaves had returned to our area. We had rescued 1,960 createds of all ages since we began. We transported 1,939 to the gathering region, the whereabouts I did not know. Twenty-one died on the way back to the cleansing tank, twelve from being drained of heart and horrible burns, and nine from my blade work. I cut too far.

Beatrice and I helped the living begin their recoveries to gain strength for transport and we grieved the deaths. We buried their free bodies properly, and were grateful at least they did not die alone, rotting inside a creature that likewise rotted when it had drained the life energy out of the created. I had brought them back dead, with their own blood drenching my tunic, our ground, and our lives. I would never know the status of the one I carried until we arrived at the holding tank. Beatrice and I had grown weary, even though we knew the need and had passion for the mission. I had become tired. I had become furious with what seemed endless and maybe even useless.

XII

I arose at 2:30 a.m. like many a night, unless sheer exhaustion or weather made hunting too dangerous or impossible. It was Saturday night, really Sunday morning, the last hunt of the week, or first I guess. Some things will always be decided by clocks and culture, which can mark and cultivate us, or control and cult-create in us. Regulate or possess. Beatrice slept soundly this night through my early movements. I preferred that she remain asleep; I needed time to sit and pray. I had learned the child pose of prayer from Beatrice years ago. Her place of prayer and mine had become the same. I drank coffee and gas water, as I sat before prayers, read paragraphs mainly from the most ancient book and prepared for war. I gathered up my clothing and headed out on a light stomach, giving more room in my lungs for air and the feeling of lightness. It was an old habit from high school when I would run early mornings when training for the decathlon in late spring. Didn't last in college. My zeal for mental obstacles took over for what had been competitive physical zeal. Now, they were both united, held together by my willingness to feel my own heart's longings that were covered in paragraphs.

It smelled like rain. I could see lightning off in the distance in the direction I was headed. I estimated it was two or three hours from us. The storm quickened my steps. I walked the familiar paths, before starting the jog. My senses had developed so far beyond the first night I was introduced to my destiny with the near loss of my life. The spiritual-emotional development, from the limbic outwards, had worked all the way through my system to the use of my senses, like a bat can see with its ears and an owl can hear with its eyes in the dark. My triune brain had integrated finely, to my own amazement, like a storybook character who could do amazing things that we assumed were fictional. The metaphor and imagination had become literal in the substance of the spiritual and emotional world. The meta was truer than the literal. Truth had overtaken reality, and yet there were two responses to this fact. Integration or deeper denial to ward off the vulnerability that truth brings. I never believed until seven years ago that these capacities could exist.

The whole hunt and rescue mission brought everywhere I had been in my life and everything that I had done to a focused desire and an active point; even the ugliness of my egotism had become mercy for the createds. I understood how it happened. But for grace, go I. As I jogged onward I thought of the loneliness I still carried within that I registered as post-existential reality. I still knew so little, so I focused again on where I headed at the moment.

I ran the paths that I had been going out on for seven years, all like spokes from a hub. The dirt paths and stones I navigated easily, entering woods west of our place, a half-mile from our back porch. A slight climb of five degrees or so for another half-mile then descended to a level surface of grasses with sporadic thickets that stretched for miles. When I came to the level, I slowed and smelled, listened and saw with my intuition. Entering a thicket I had yet to explore, I felt about the roots of the thickest trunks of trees first before moving to smaller and smaller growth, occasional lightning giving me quick pictures. The search was all about the root and water source. The creatures supplied just enough sap from the trees to keep their symbiotic survival extended by feeding the createds on pure instinct. They fed off of the createds, all safe and sound underground, avoiding any threat.

Everything about the weather, humidity, the soft rhythm of the crickets, even an early mockingbird song reminded me of so many summer evenings or early mornings of our past; plopped down in a chair in our courtyard after a day of working on our place. Our sons coming in from somewhere or jogging in from a workout on the mountain, the grill lit and ready for fish or steaks. A nighthawk swooshing by at dusk and then the moon rising. I would always notice the crickets.

The moss underneath my boots cushioned every move I made as I entered the next thicket, still thinking of those days. I remembered Beatrice and me lying on the soft moss one afternoon in a thicket near our home; the past and what I was doing at this moment ripped inside of me.

I turned to go to the next tree, heard a thunder peal echo in the distance, and then bumped into a creature above ground just as lightning flashed to outline its grotesque form. My heart rate overtook my whole system as the memory of being slashed up in the hole seven years ago flashed before my eyes. Pulling my dagger before I could form another thought, I slit the passageway of the creature. It didn't move; stood paralyzed and was dead. I heard its breath come out when I bumped it and then nothing when I slit its throat. I could see its arms in the next flash of lightning, stretched out towards me, claws out, its gut jutted out like a giant mole on its hind legs as thunder banged closer to the thicket. It had no eyes. I kicked it over, breathing hard in my fear. I would swear its razor sharp paws were in a pose of pleading, prepared for termination—if it could even think of such things—before I slit its throat. The sewage stench of its inner rot met my nostrils as it dropped to the ground. I thought I heard a sigh when it hit, like a human finding relief of rest rather than a hissing sound a compressor makes letting out air. I quickly gathered myself, found a hole that had to be nearby, and dropped quickly into the hole beside the carcass. There was little phosphorescent glow from the dead creature, which confused me as I dropped in.

My breathing was coming much too fast, adrenaline flowing in, meeting the unexpected in the insanity that had become normal. I needed to stop and listen, but before I could, lightning struck again, illuminating the entrance for a second and where I was standing. I faced six creatures with claws out towards me as I started slashing wildly at the throats I could place from the seconds of lightning, protecting myself and wondering what was happening. I hit six quickly and moved towards a seventh as lightning flashed again. I moved towards it fast, suddenly seeing a set of eyes flash light, changed my knife on sheer history and gutted it, not knowing if I cut the heart or not. I could hardly fathom the fact that I had not slit its throat.

I broke protocol, which tested to see how much life was left in the created, and "birthed" it in the tunnel, not caring what would happen next or if I would be attacked from the side or back. I just didn't care. I carried its limp and emaciated body toward the opening in my arms, the stench making me vomit on the created and my tunic. It glowed with the burning phosphorous. Before I climbed out, I slid the greasy form into the pouch on my back, seeing its eyes open slightly as its face passed mine when lightning struck again. The sigh I heard sounded so low and painful, I was sure the night would be no more than a slaughter and another mercy death for one of our own.

As I reached the surface of the earth, I heard another sigh, what would have been a grunt of pain had there been enough energy. I could hear either breath or a whispering for its life, all of it running together in the broken groaning, because I was groaning, too, and breathing hard as lightning hit again and thunder close behind. The wind picked up and I started running hard, running from the rain I knew would catch us and the grief I could never get away from. I ran hard and raised my face to the sky, all the reveries of the moss a thousand miles away. I bellowed my hatred of everything dark and cruel, everything I had become a part of. The rain came hard, blowing against my back. I ran harder, screaming for the created to live. "You live; you hear me, you live! You've got to live," as my feet hit the ground hard and quick, fighting to get home.

I felt its head bounce back and forth as I cut left and right on the trail home. It was so light; I reached one time to make sure I wasn't in a nightmare. It had no hold on my back, its feet not in the stirrups, legs bumping against my thighs. I ran like my life depended on it. All I could think was "live" over and over again. An animal growl rolled up out of me again; I wanted to stop and start crying, fall on the ground and stay. "You live; you've got to live!" I cried as I saw the lights of home in the distance. Somehow I picked up speed, hearing the rain pelting against my helmet and tunic, water washing over the created, no telling how long it had been since it had felt rain. My lungs burned as I neared the cleansing area, legs heavy like lead, as I collapsed at Beatrice's waiting hands and feet. I didn't even see her face, as I fell forward, nothing left.

I could feel her work the created out of the pouch on

my back. The rain beat on the tin roof, the lantern on the ground near my face. I started weeping when my breath came back to me, exhausted at all the love lost. I was slowly pulling up on to all fours trying to stay on course when I heard Bea gasp. I raised my head slowly towards her voice and looked straight into the starved face of my brother. I crawled towards the tank, two feet and ten years from the last time I had seen him. Reaching out an exhausted shaking hand, I touched the side of his face and then placed my forehead against his ashen cheek. I gently pulled him softly to my shoulder and wept and wept, so tired, so damned tired. He could not speak and I didn't want to. Bea's hand rested on my head, stroking my hair for how long I do not know as she slowly rinsed cleansing water over my brother and me.

"Please live; please live, my brother; please live!" I cried as I held him.

I heard a whisper. My ear was so close to his mouth. I heard him gasp, trying desperately to speak. He knew me. I listened hard, looking into his face with his head cradled in my open hands. He said very slowly, hoarsely and very distinctly, one word, "advocate," before he slipped more completely into the warm water and Bea's hands, barely alive, finally resting in silence and salvation.

We bathed him quietly, with few words between us. We had to scrape his skin in several places where pus and acid had built up, attacking like barnacles on a ship hull. He made not one sound while the water recycled in the tank and

the rain continued over the next hour, thunder and lightning along with it.

XIII

————

My throat became tighter and tighter over the next hour. My jaws more and more set. Fury struck a stalemate between my throat, my clenched teeth and my shattered heart.

Beatrice and I lifted my brother from the water and wrapped his warped and scarred body in a drying blanket. We then carried him into our recovery wing, a large room with a windowed wall that looked out over the meadow. It used to be our family gathering room for us and our guests. That time seemed so dimly lit now. The room has four beds, one bed already occupied by another created resting easily after two days of restoration. The room is clean, white and warm, green stone tiles on the floor, yet very much a convalescent place—recovery, restoration, replenishment, re-creation, then transport to the next place. We help until strength to depart is accomplished, but I already don't want to let go of Josh now that he is found—if he lives. Beatrice's greatest strengths take over in this place. Part perseverance, a history of experience with death and life, and passion for the return of a being to who they are made to be, move her about in quiet, surrendered assurance, the same way I hunt. Beatrice would begin to spoon-feed drops of a molecularly adjusted broth to Josh, unless he couldn't take it in. He was the first created I had ever delivered in a tunnel, and so his weakness would be a mark against the strength of his heart that would have to remain desperate for liberation.

I asked Bea if she would be good for a while. I told her I wanted to work on the stone wall of the flower bed we had started, where we planned to plant lilies in the fall. We wanted to see their blooms trumpet in the sun when they bloomed at the field's edge. That dream seemed just that only; the rock pile had been waiting on me for seven years. The inanimate frames life, and therefore, has voice in the frame. She looked at me confused, quizzically, saw the rain still hitting the windows, and then with trust. She knew something was up, and nodded to me with understanding as she looked into my hard-set eyes.

I walked out to the cleaning trough, stripped down to nothing, then soaked and rinsed boots, tunic, pants, helmet, knife and sheath of the detritus of how we had been living. I slung everything on drying hooks near the heater for the water, not even finishing the usual ritual of oiling the dagger after cleaning. I stuck it in a post and walked to the back porch that had become our changing room. I dried off there, changed into my gardening pants, old leather work boots, t-shirt and grabbed some leather gloves as I pushed out the screen door, and then pulled the back door tightly shut.

The rain had let up some, but I would be soaked again soon. The clouds still looked as thick as a dark gray wall, no break in them, no light. At the edge of the meadow, I jumped the three feet off of the retaining wall from our backyard where the rock pile and flowerbed were, almost falling in the wet dirt pile when I landed. The wall had been half finished and needed another fifteen yards of stacked stone, two and a half feet or so tall. Another bed on the other side of the steps that came down into the meadow from the rise in the back-yard had been completed years ago. Its lily blooms drooped in the rain and wind. I was going to finish the wall today.

I bent over the rock pile and picked the first one that would fit well. This pile of stone had not been touched since I fell through the looking glass and couldn't escape. The rain started harder, right on cue. The lightning struck somewhere nearby, and the thunder rolled. I didn't look up. After an hour or so, I had to hold my gloves up to let the water drain out of them. My boots began to stick in the mud from the rut I had made walking back and forth from the pile of stone. I never stopped moving. I used the rusted rock hammer that I found just where I had left it, intending to return the next day I'm sure. Shaping any rock that didn't fit tightly in the dry stack, I swung the hammer hard, rock chips splintering away, stacked it and moved on. I wanted to stop thinking, make it all stop. Finish something. Make one damn flower-bed and notice the lilies as they bloom. I wanted to cut the grass and complain about it, worry about it not raining or the weeds coming up in the yard, worry about the air conditioner not cooling enough, or wonder about whether or not we had charcoal for the cooker so we could hang out in the evening.

The lightning struck nearer and I screamed at it all. "Just kill me; I dare you. I'm not walking off this flowerbed. I'm planting lilies when the time comes after I fill the bed with dirt—just as soon as it dries out. You bet I am!" I mumbled more dares without even looking up. I wanted my simple common life back. My legs started getting heavier, my dares grew less infused with daring, my boots were more mud than leather and saturated to the point that water squished out of them when I walked. I had been soaked since 3:30 am and hadn't eaten since the night before. And I still just didn't care, but I couldn't move much faster anymore. The thunder pealed loudly, and I could feel the ground shake under my feet, but the delay was longer after the lightning strike.

I still wasn't leaving and the wall was finished and I wasn't dead. "Kill me; I'm not leaving," I said quietly, then loudly as I collapsed in a sitting position on the wall behind the lily bed, my muddy boots in the empty space that needed dirt and flowers. I groaned quietly, breathed in deeply and began to cry again. One more out there—my sister, probably dead. My brother, Josh emaciated unto death. I wanted to kill all the lizards, moles, or whatever they were. I wanted to kill death and despair, even as I felt the pull into them. I wanted blood, some place to bring revenge against everything that had no heart while I hated my own and wished it banished to darkness. I was done and wept about how done I was, savagely done with all of this, hating all the apathy that I so desperately wanted and would not and could not take any more. The apathy had made us all susceptible to become the grotesque as creatures or the Collective, or probably some other form I had not yet seen. I just groaned quietly.

I saw myself as alone, alone with the burden of the knowledge Bea and I carried, and wanting to save the people who had been swallowed, but I just didn't have anything left—even if I ate and rested. The hunting was over, the creatures were starving and the createds would be drained to death, stop and rot inside the scaly stench of the creatures, a sewage grave, a casket of hair, scales, empty bones, and poisoned razors. Only the razors would eventually be left below the ground as the ground would slowly sink and the trees would grow again as a testimony to death and life. I was finished.

XIV

————

I slowly looked up across the meadow and saw the backstop we had built and let out a snort and shook my head slightly. The rain had stopped. I recognized when I raised my head that where I sat and how I lived was life as it is, really is and that I could no more leave my passion than say my sons had never existed or stop loving Beatrice or hate liberty for that matter. I advocate. Others advocate. That is what we do. We are a voice for the silent until they are validated to have their own, so they can do the same.

I put my right hand on my knee and pushed my torso up straight, still looking at the ground. I pulled my gloves off and dropped them where I was looking. The fingers of the leather stayed curled in the shape of hands bent to work, stiff with mud, rain and sweat. When I lifted my head and saw the backstop at the far edge of the meadow again, I let out the slightest breath of mockery in the recognition of how far we all were from where we thought we were headed years ago and where we wound up. Hope in what was, indeed, was gone. Hope in what we were doing was just barely alive.

Advocate. My brother knew the word and used it deliberately, somehow having presence of heart enough to be able to whisper it as his last word or his first one. To intercede as defender. He would also understand the word convalescence: to grow strong, the inceptive of growing strong again, or well. In Roman law it meant to become valid. That is exactly what could happen now, as Josh became fully human again, to gain his voice, perhaps his dreams and the passion to move towards them, if he could live again.

Just thinking of the words, themselves, tired me because they were no longer just words. They had become actions, and had living, breathing realities more alive by hands and hearts than any substance in definition.

The definition became the action or not. Yet I had no action left in me for now.

I stared again at the backstop and the memories of past lives, and then I heard a whisper, as quiet as a lullaby goodnight or a slight breeze in a pine tree.

I didn't turn my head until I heard it again, the sound of my name. I then slowly turned to the whisper to see my father sitting beside me on the stone wall. He had just said, "Abe," as he spoke to me the third time. My eyes travelled up his frame to his face. His cordovan wing tips shined like always. One of his hands was up in the air, as he finished speaking, the hands of a surgeon, and his eyes much softer than I remember, still gray, and still strong. Beside him sat my grandfather, flannel tartan shirt, buttoned up to the top, respectfully, like he wore at birthday parties and Friday night suppers. His face was remarkable because his sight was restored. He had had a glass eye since the time I had known him; he had lost his vision in a farming accident. A tree limb had hit him across the face when they had been cutting fence posts and took his left eye. His expression was quiet and caring. I had not seen my father since the night I had rushed him to the hospital. He died on the operating table; I understood that he was still giving orders about his treatment as they were putting him under.

I had not seen my grandfather for 22 years. His death had crushed my father; something was not finished between them. It actually seemed OK now, though. Another man stood a few feet beyond them and a little out front. I recognized the large man, Benjamin, from pictures I had seen. He was my great-grandfather. He had on a straw hat, a cigar in his mouth and a thick drooping mustache, and wore well-oiled brogans. He also wore a tie that came down not much farther than his sternum.

I did not move, too tired to even be shocked. Nothing really surprised me anymore. My capacity to accept reality and struggle with the truth had expanded exponentially. I was struck, however, by how much I missed my father; I didn't move because I knew I would get mud all over his clean white shirt. He looked at me with seriousness and a slight, crooked grin and then pulled me to him gently. After releasing me and smiling at the mud all over his side and shoulder, he began to talk slowly and deliberately. "So many things never got said. There aren't enough words right now to say how sorry I am for what I missed with you and how much you had to go learn without me. I am sorry, and I want you to know that you are not alone. I am sorry, too, for the failure that has you in this horrible place right now. We all are." I looked towards the other two who nodded imperceptibly as my father continued.

"We did not speak or act on what we knew and saw coming. We, I, am part of the aloneness of everything now. You and the others, more than you know, are shifting the balance one person at a time. Now is all you have; the only place of action is now." He looked into my face searching my eyes and with the compassion that many a patient had given themselves to in the midst of their personal crises.

"You are doing well going forward and halting in neutral. You have no reverse. The ancients commend you and urge you to press forward. Stay in. The worlds have collided. The spiritual has increased its teleological speed and the circles are tightening. Biology—emotion—spirit—have only lately emerged and converged in ways that have transmorphed metaphor into what you have historically called reality. Now, metaphor, reality, myth, and truth move in and out of spheres no longer compartmentalized. The war of love for it all has come. You see, like I would not, that the emotional and spiritual were always meant to transcend biology. The world of power and control, the drawing into voidition, you called it, work against life. Society is not tending; it is pretending. It is not contending; it is controlling. Stay in, Abe, now."

His facial expression bore sadness of a heart laden with loss. He looked the way he did the night he told me about trying to save his father after he was brought into the emergency room one night when he himself was on call. The powerlessness in love slams us so hard into the questions that I wonder how the impact doesn't kill us all. He couldn't save his father then, and he couldn't save me now.

"You are not alone," he said again, and those were the last words I would hear him speak, as he looked past my face with imploring seriousness and some form of blessing. I followed his eyes, my neck turning stiffly to my right. Both of my sons looked straight at me, into me even, with the same sense of pride my father had offered me. They stood beside me ready to pounce as their solemn faces took on the joy and movement of a long, long absence. They jumped at me, pulled me to my feet and the muddy embrace filled me as we held each other yelling until I just leaned into them as we breathed deeply and quietly resting on each other. Our heads rested together for a bit before they plopped me back down and we all looked at each other. I got them muddier as they leaned over me and my arms went around them. Eight years, and miles, depths, changes, and tumult had passed among us since we had seen each other. The letters they sent that I had always assumed were hyperbole or some form of symbols I could now let them know in person how much I know they have done to save a lot of imprisoned createds.

They looked hard and serious, so alive and solid. They wore navy tunics of thick cotton and well-worn leather breeches, boots laced up to the knees the color of the pants, a dagger sheathed in each boot. I looked at their hardness questioningly. "You taught us more than you know, Dad," my youngest said. My oldest nodded with kindness that humbled me. His shoulders bore thick muscles as he was grounded with strength. The youngest appeared more like twisted rebar and wide shoulders. They both carried an attitude of inner passion. They looked at each other then and shook hands with joy, and bear hugged as I realized they had not seen each other in eight years. They had the gravitas of warriors and the freedom of heart to be themselves.

And I had attempted to stop them from stepping into their quests. We had argued harshly. I told them that they were being tempestuous and overwrought with wanting to do anything even if it was wrong. I had wounded them, telling them that they weren't ready, that the threats were all exaggerated about the Collective. They tried to tell me what they had seen and felt. I accused the oldest of leading his brother into unnecessary danger, that they needed to wait, stay patient. Beatrice had cried, telling me to stop, how out of line I was, even as she herself feared for their safety. We had raised them not to seek the mediocre, but to declare themselves as free of heart, "to climb the mountain of their dreams and hold the flag brave and true," she had yelled my own words at me. I had stared at her hard, with fierce hatred, not able to live what I believed at the time.

I had walked from the house, run up the trails, realizing how frightened I was, that I had not prepared them, and when they were harmed, it would all be on me. I had been compromised for years, attempting to walk on top of the fence across the fires on either side. I had talked liberty as an idea, not really knowing or believing in the costs. When I came down from the trails, they were gone. Like a wound that ripped my heart through the middle, I sat down to hear Bea tell me that she had let them go. Our letters could never heal the wound that their presence in all our times brought to this moment. And not until I had been released to having to decide, did I begin to become who they had been raised to be. Bea had never stopped loving me, but not until seven years ago could she fully give herself to me. I wasn't home to myself or her. Neither the youngest nor the oldest had ever shoved my words, all those caustic words, in my face. They had believed beyond my fears and lived the truth.

I noticed something over their shoulders, and they turned in the same direction. Just beyond them were three lighted adumbrations that flickered against the gray horizon and dark woods. Three human shapes, light-filled and thick with luminescence appeared to look our way, nod and raise a hand to us. They were no more than six feet away. My oldest son repeated what my father said as if he weren't surprised at all by the shapes, light and movement. "You are not alone," he said with a thick tone. "None of us are who are known from within. Dad, it all comes together, but we don't decide how it ends. We will indeed see you again."

I felt another pang of heartache, exhausted as I was because his face already told the story of departure. I heard a high-pitched tone coming from the woods behind me towards the house, and turned to look, saw nothing, looked again, and recognized a man walking out of the trees playing a wooden flute. I turned back to my people, but they were gone.

XV

I looked up towards the horizon above the hills. The clouds were broken by the light coming through the cracks. I could hear the croaking of the frogs in the wet areas to the south. I was certain they had talked to me. I was sure of what I had just seen. I had been found; I was not alone. I was tired and hungry, and the wall for the lily bed was finally finished. All real.

That man with the flute certainly could be a hallucination though, but not one I wanted. He kept playing as he walked in my direction, like he knew what he was doing, but took his time doing it. The whining of the flute was a B flat tune that came slow and mournful to me, like a plaintive ballad. He had not signified that he had seen me, and I wished he wouldn't, such a strange bird he already appeared to be. But I couldn't help but watch his approach, wary and unwelcoming.

He stopped playing for some seconds to pull up his baggy, stained, cache pants that sagged miserably at the waist. Then, he reached up to push his glasses back up the bridge of his nose before beginning to play again, exactly where he had left off. I could see the flute was bamboo.

He walked within four feet of me, ended on a fading note, and looked at me, having come down into the mud to be in front of me at eye level, though I was sitting. The smell of kerosene, which I assumed his pants were stained with, and clove filled my nose, so pungent that the air around me took on the whole atmosphere of him. Holding his flute under his arm, he pulled up his pants the second time, tucked his faded denim shirt in, and pushed his glasses up his nose again as he looked at me, like he was standing at a front door preparing to meet someone for the first time.

After a few seconds of him staring at me, examining would be the more appropriate word, but never taking his eyes off mine, I decided that I was seeing things and had decided to try to move towards the house and find my sanity. This figment made me doubt everything I had just seen. Just as I began to move, he pointed the flute towards my face. "Handmade," he said in a twangy, Scottish sounding accent. He sounded like he looked—sun blanched skin, sandy hair, cut close to the head, blue-green eyes that looked tired, if not haunted, conflicted by a mouth appearing to say something he thinks amusing, unkempt, unpretentious, talented, if not brilliant, or crazy, and frankly, just out of sorts was all I could think as I looked back at this very real person. I couldn't make him up if I had tried. "Bamboo, no nodes at all. The worst playing flutes have nodes. Seasoned bamboo and seasoned oil. B flat makes the sound for all of our tunes, I would say," he said. He didn't stop there. "I used hot iron pointers to burn the holes. Write all my own tunes. Like I say, B flat plays the truth for us; plaintive."

His roundish eyes took on multiple expressions as he spoke, but the watching from them didn't stop while he talked. If he were an enemy, I was dead already. "Who are you?" I muttered with my eyes squinting up into his face because the sun was breaking through the clouds, keeping my head up as long as I could. He sat on the wall in front of me when my head dropped, my neck sore from dehydration. "He is gracious," I thought.

"Do not ask for whom the bell tolls; it tolls for thee," he said with solid execution, and then he went on to say, "Death be not proud, but indeed it does sting. The metaphysical poets were definitely on to something. But they didn't see this mess, did they?" he snickered and then smirked, still not giving me a name or a purpose.

He then reached toward me with his handmade flute and tapped me on the forehead easily, saying, "I'm going to be your friend. Something, I daresay, you do not know a great deal about, beyond your words, your paragraphs, and your books, 'til this very moment. I'm going to be your friend. Yep. I choose you, friend. Doubles the joy and halves the sorrows. I'm the guy who has your back, you see," making his mouth crooked and bringing an old New York accent to a deep voice, then back to his twang. "And because I have your back, you got to have mine. See, we battle back to back. Nothing can get us that way, at least not so easily. I'll have your front, too, like now, talking to you clear and straight. I'm going to be your right and left arm, too, and say into your ear, 'this is the way; walk in it.'

"I'm the best friend you will ever have because I'm going to make sure you get home to Beatrice or at least die trying. We are going to finish this mission. You cannot do this alone and I'm going to call you to changes you cannot see so you can love that woman up there in the house better. You see, as a man sees in the water, his own reflection is not enough. You can see in a friend's face the truth of your own heart.

"Aristotle said it well, if I might repeat myself, 'A friend will double your joy and halve your sorrows.' I liked it better when I thought Papa invented that one. I certainly have room for another friend. That's my speech and every word of it is true." He stood, cinched his pants up, neglected his shirt since we had been introduced, sort of, and pushed his glasses back up his nose. "By the way, Doctor sent me," he said offhandedly, just as I was about to believe in magic. I looked at his bedraggled appearance, always loved that word "bedraggled," and I was confounded by his infectious peculiarity.

"Years ago you fell into a hole. The doctor who stitched you and introduced you to such a life of love, mentioned me," snickering at his sarcasm. "I'm the fellow two hills over outside your region to the north and west. I met Doctor a couple of years before you did. Remember, you had never seen him and Beatrice didn't really know him, though she had seen him before when she worked there some. He roams, a bit, I'll say. I met him the same way you did. Cut all about my legs. Had the squirts ever since—toxicity; that's how come I don't wear a belt, case I need to get them down quick. Haven't found an herb or oil, no homeopathic cure yet. Don't believe it's physical anyway, ultimately, you see," which I didn't really, but I knew he was headed somewhere familiar and interesting, as "my friend" as yet with no name continued. "We are officially living in the times when emotion, our inner states, translate into our biological results. Not cause our biological results, not etiology, mind you, not at all; it's development. I'm telling you, translate, like one language and another language communicate the same thing but seem different; this same thing is occurring with emotional-spiritual-physio-biological languages.

"It's reverse transudation, like how the pores open to exude sweat to cool the body for its good, except backwards. This is reverse; the pores of the skin open to turn the body against itself according to the heart's will. Like owners look like their dogs eventually. The transubstantiation of absorbing things into your being with the will's intent to stop the heart from experiencing its power to feel and need. The price of pain and cost of vulnerability is real, Dr. Philology. We thought we could escape it.

"A person wills or determines to do whatever necessary to remain hidden emotionally and spiritually, with the result that the will opens the 'pores' of being." He excitedly and quickly made the hand motions of quote marks when

109

he said, "pores" and then moved right on excitedly like he had never been able to speak these things before. "I'm telling you, we have come to the place at which a spiritual rupture occurred because the heart was rejected. Insane, huh?" he asked, obviously rhetorically because he went right on, picking the flute up that he dropped when he cinched his pants up again and pushed his glasses up, without barely a break in speech. Yet his eyes were looking for me with many questions, I thought searching to see if I could keep up. "We believed we finally could escape it, and the sickness is the ego covering of the true self these folks volunteered for, and they absorbed the biological reverse transudation of their own refusal of heart. Crazy, but it's the facts.

It is not a new story about us, but the effects are changing, literally transforming our bio-physiological makeup, but for one thing. It can use the heart but not change it; thus, the createds can come back to life, much more desirous of life as it is made to be. Like people recreated by having tasted death and despair; the heart isn't made for those things." I looked hard at him when he used those words, "death and despair" because I knew them to be real; I had heard Doctor speak them, and the antidote for the poison in them. The createds did have a new humility and new capacities to live and love, a new strength we once called character and had assumed it could carry on without being fed. Even in spite of their trauma, which I assumed the next place would assist them in healing, a regenerating seemed to be occurring even before they were transported from our place.

"Everything is speeding up. The spiritual evolution, of course, would move faster because it appears not to have substance, like the speed of light versus the movement of a glacier. Instead of epochs, we must talk of years and soon weeks and days. The very atmosphere of their own wills swallowed them, and then the creature that resulted sucked the heart dry—to death. The Collective knows, too. Out of sight, out of mind. They only let us live because we are quiet, and seem to have no impact. They have no idea of the rescues, the transporting or the plan. That would get us noticed.

Keep it simple; owners look like their dogs," he said and stopped talking suddenly, looking at me quizzically. I heard everything he said, and I still was trying to place his accent; Appalachian-Scottish was all I could come up with. I was too tired to respond, emotionally spent even more than physically.

"Sorry, my friend," he suddenly said, noticing how unfocused I seemed. "What kind of a friend am I proving to be so far? I went on a bit, didn't I?" he asked without a question again. He said, "I'm so excited to meet you and about what we are going to do. Let me help you to the house. Beatrice knows I'm here. She is quite glad you have a new friend. I'll explain more on the fortnight when you and I meet."

"Yes, brilliant as I had thought earlier, and I would add presumptuous to the list," I thought such things about him. I knew nothing about a meeting with this friend-stranger some night soon.

"Like I say," he continued as he reached his arms under mine and pulled me to my feet, with a strength that surprised me for a man of any size. "My, my, you weigh more than I had calculated with the dehydration and two missed meals. Your muscle has kept you going, too. Good for you," he chortled. The man just didn't stop. "Like I say," he continued again. I now logically decided that he had a severe neurological disorder that wouldn't allow him to stop talking or be still, or what used to be called bipolarism, and he had moved into a manic phase. But my heart knew differently.

"Friends have more eyes to help us see," he said. "My Papa did say that one. No Aristotle in that one. Closer to Plato, who by the way, came close to suggesting some of the spiritual dimensions of which we speak," he said as we turned to the house. I was steady on my feet, but the boots were still heavy with mud. I almost laughed when he said, "of which we speak" because there had been no "we" in the speaking, unless he used the royal "we," meaning he. "Here you go," he said as we moved towards the house slowly, me weakly scraping my heavy boots on the ground, and him pulling his pants up and pushing his glasses back in place.

XVI

———

"Plato steered off course severely because the Greeks kept discounting the heart's knowledge and placed Reason alone up on the pedestal of mystery, the mystery we are made to live. Aristotle, for all of his wisdom, moved us even farther away from the invisible. Then, the discourse became all about Reason, more than what it speaks to." He finally stopped talking as we walked. He placed a hand on my left shoulder for a few soft pats as a gesture of comfort and kindness as we walked. After some quiet steps, he placed the flute to his mouth and played five, long sorrowful notes. "That finishes the tune I started. Always finish," he said quietly, even wistfully, like the notes. He then put his flute in his back pocket, and we walked back to the house without another word spoken. "Not crazy at all," I thought. "Brilliant, and in need of a friend, too."

As we came to the windows of the convalescent room, my friend shaded his eyes to see into the window. He waved when he saw Beatrice. She had lit a candle and sat near the bed of the other created, Rachel, while she ate a thick soup, loaded with amino acid supplements and organic vegetables for rich flavor and nourishment. Josh slept on his back under covers neatly tucked around him, his arms resting along each side on top of the covers. His face looked peaceful, but for his mouth, which had a grim appearance. I felt refreshed somehow and very hungry.

Beatrice came out to us just as I said, "thank you" to the man. As Beatrice arrived, he shook her hand and they smiled appreciatively to each other.

"Williams," he said to Bea. "William Williams."

Bea said smiling, "Good name for such a peculiar man."

"Nice to meet you, William Williams," I added as I reached out to shake his hand.

"Yes, 'peculiar,'" he said. "It means uniquely one's own; unique to one's self, as I'm sure you know, my dear philologist, so thank you for the compliment to my freedom and to yours and Beatrice's and those two createds in there if they will receive it," as he pointed through the windows towards the Rachel and Josh.

"As I depart, I am reminded of love," William suddenly said. And then he spoke the following words so conversationally that they seemed as every day as the encore of the setting sun. "Place me like a seal over your heart, like a seal on your arm; for love is as strong as death, its jealousy unyielding as the grave. It burns like a blazing fire, like a mighty flame. Many waters cannot quench love; rivers cannot wash it away. If one were to give all the wealth of his house for love, it would be utterly scorned. Those words Papa didn't speak either, but he believed them. Solomon got those specific ones, but he was just reporting what he knew and what he experienced. Love is not reasonable, but it makes absolute sense.

"I will see you, Abe, in three nights around midnight. Beatrice has the directions. Beatrice will, again, handle the createds care while you are on an early dawn hunt, but you do not need your dagger for this one. Leave it here."

Those words frightened me terribly. I realized that I had not left our property past dark without the dagger in years. I looked at Williams questioningly, but he continued on. "Josh will heal in body. The heart as you know takes longer. I was a neurophysiologist in the other life before I rediscovered the profound music of life's symphony, starting with the backbeat that I had become deaf to. You know, we recuse ourselves of the music of life, the very symphonic heart of it, its color, its rhythmic beat of passion to intimacy with its unavoidably awe-inspiring integrity through which we develop." He stopped abruptly, realizing that he had gone on again, then sighed. He did have room for a friend. I wondered if the man had not talked in years. I wondered about his own loneliness.

He abruptly waved at both of us, while standing at arm's length, pulled his pants up and took his flute out of his back pocket, adjusted his glasses, and turned to walk away. He was playing his flute after four or five unhurried steps back towards home as he disappeared into the woods heading northwest, the smell of kerosene and clove going with him.

Bea smiled slightly and her eyes showed a celebration within them. She took my hand as we entered the back porch. I sat on the bench just inside the door, pulling off my socks with my boots left outside. I stripped down to my drawers, with Bea leaning against the doorjamb into our kitchen, smiling even bigger than earlier. I hung up the muddy clothes on pegs to dry some, and couldn't help but smile back at her in spite of everything, the craziness of it all. Today had been a great day, even though the clock no longer marked the timing of things.

"You shower, then let's eat. What a wilder day than we could even dream, from nightmare to wonderful goodness all spilling everywhere. Your brother is sleeping like a baby. He will make it, Abe," she said with her arms now folded under her breasts and her face showing clear confidence. I heard her voice more than I noticed her face. Her whole being struck me wonderfully when she tucked her hair behind her ear. "I don't think he knows yet where he is or that he truly exists. I suspect he thinks he is dreaming."

I stood up and headed towards her. She then said, "We are blessed with this life; it is tiring and scary, and devastating, and truly normal. Even though we have lost the expected, even the predictable, and horror creeps about, we know the truth; we are free, and we make a difference; I love you, Abe." Tears filled her eyes as I came within a breath of her. "We are so alive, and you have never looked so marvelously normal to me than you do right now," she whis-

116

pered. I put my hands on her cheeks, placed my forehead on hers, then slid my arms down her back and pulled her to me, standing in the doorway of our kitchen in wet drawers.

I showered as quickly as I could, and returned to the kitchen, the smell of whole grain pancakes and eggs filling me up already. I opened the cold box and grabbed some grilled chicken and grapes to complete the meal. I filled clear glasses with blue rims full of fresh spring water, and dropped mint leaves into them. She brought a white platter of the food to the table, still steaming. I had already put the honey and butter on the table. We ate well and long; the candles burned low before we finished. We sat close to each other, our thighs touching as we talked, exchanging glances that went far beyond our words.

We remembered our lives, sitting at the table like we used to do sometimes when the boys were still here, and we watched storms cross the sky and the day close on the meadow and our hills. I told her everything of the day, from finding Josh and what happened in the tunnel to William Williams tapping me on the forehead. She laughed at that loudly, and said that she was glad I had a new friend, with just a little mocking in her voice, but I knew how much she meant it. We talked a long time about our sons, how full they looked, how she would recognize her boys but would be struck by the thickness of their bearings, now. They had seen and experienced much. I healed with them I told her. I told her that they had become exactly what she knew they were made to be when I didn't have the courage to let them go.

I reached my hand to her hair and leaned to her face to kiss her forehead and cheeks and her lips that received my mouth gently. She whispered to me, "I love you, Abe. I'm so thankful that we live on the water and our boat is not grounded on the beach. We cast off years ago. Do you remember the words, 'We ride in the currents of a quest' from the paper you wrote years ago? You have made them true. We do not 'live fully in an adventure,' you wrote, 'which means to venture out and return,'" she smiled, knowing my obsession with words. But she went on, "'we live fully in a quest, which means to push off shore with no intention of coming back.' I have never forgotten those words. I was just never sure we would live them."

She leaned into me and kissed my cheek and neck, as I then brought her mouth to mine again. The moonlight shined into the windows and the candles' light faded out. I took her hand and pulled her to me as we stood. I led her to the cleansing tank, the waters steam rising to the night sky. The water had filtered clean again and the eucalyptus and aloe scent was pungent in the evening humidity. I took off my shirt while watching her do the same; we entered the cleansing waters together and disappeared in its healing while the moon lit our night, and shadowed our future. Her skin glowed in the presence of the night, and I gave myself to the deep pools of her olive eyes.

XVII

The next morning I sat quietly in a wicker chair near my sleeping brother. Rachel slept soundly just behind me. Her health had progressed dramatically since yesterday, Josh's first day. She used to be beautiful and, we hoped, would be again. She would be leaving in two days. The transport came once a week in the cover of the night. Josh lay on his back still in the same position as the night before. We had fed Josh before we went to bed, and Rachel fed herself after we brought it to her. She had quietly asked about Josh, beginning to care beyond herself. She asked if he would live, seeing how terribly weak he appeared to be. Little did she realize that she had started similarly four days earlier.

I watched Josh breathe and watched his face closely. The stillness of his sleep and the calmness of his breathing conflicted with the physical condition of his convalescence. His right hand occasionally gripped the cover in a fist and then would relax again; his face would cloud in a grimace, then pass like a cloud under the sun. He struggled to return, to see that he had left a place that would never leave him completely—both a curse and a blessing. He must never forget.

Seven years ago we had moved all the furniture from this once well-appointed room but for two black walnut armoires, a large Persian rug that covered the dark green tile, and a mural of the Battle of Thermopylae that scrolled across almost the entire east wall on the opposite side of the windows. The rest of the materials were well-organized recovery tools, from hot water boilers to gauze wrappings on shelves. We had also left a bust of George Washington on a granite pedestal. Bea and I had found the bust in a Paris warehouse while exploring there years back. It was under and behind lamps, boxes, and upholstered chairs. It sat on the floor, lost to where it needed to be. We shipped it to our home, never discovering its age or how it came to Paris. He remained my Cincinnatus.

I had removed the shades that had once blocked the western sun from the room. Never would this room have false darkness in it again. The light of day brought the greatest peace and regenerative strength to our passengers. It had great potency beyond our scientifically arranged and homeopathic enriched foods and drinks that we gave the createds. I glanced at the mural and remembered what a testimony of courage it spoke of when the few gave their lives to defend what lay behind them, their people and homeland. It had faded in the sun's light and would eventually come apart. Still, we left it to remind us of the courage we were all innately born to grow. I gave almost everything to life now.

My brother breathed a sigh, as I looked back into his face from the mural. He looked young like when I would get him up on summer mornings. We would eat cereal; sometimes we would make scrambled eggs and toast, with honey or jam. I never lost my attachment to eggs and toast; I smiled. We decided to start drinking coffee then, too. Sometimes our older sister, Leslee, would join us when she didn't have to be at the pool too early. She was a lifeguard and would become a swimmer for the Americas. She swam 300 days a year, so we rarely saw her in the summers, until late in the day.

Most summer days before workdays took us away, Josh and I headed for the ball fields. Usually enough of the fellas would be there to get a game up, even if we had to have a rotating batter from the field of one team. If no ball, then we headed to the spring near a decaying mansion, or down to the square where shop owners might want something hauled in or cleaned up. We would usually spend the money we earned on the square before going home.

The best days were the baseball games. Josh would usually pitch for both teams. He could throw three pitches by the time he was twelve. I smiled remembering him standing on the mound, shaking off pitches like Juan Comerro of the Southern Nationals from the West South Americas' region.

I was lost in memory staring at Josh's face when I realized his eyes had opened. He had the slightest smile on his face, too. I imagined that we had been in the same memory. I looked into his eyes for the second time in nine years, years I wished to forget; but this moment I wanted seared into my heart. Our parting had not been dramatic or memorable. We got older, made decisions, accomplished things, and drifted apart, unremarkably.

The joints of his elbows were pronounced because of profound muscle atrophy, the starvation of feeding off himself. His hands were large in appearance compared to the tiny wrists, like all the new createds. I had never seen a recovery beyond our convalescent refuge. The creature had almost finished feeding and my brother's eyes would have soon been closed. How close I had come to finishing his life, never knowing who was in the creature I stopped. I was trying to stop voidition in my rage, and that brought me close to joining exactly what I despised.

In a flash of recognition, I had seen the dim light of his eyes, righted the path of my dagger and by grace saved my brother. Never again would my own self-destruction make me like that again. I was not alone. This war was bigger than me and not a loss even if I don't make it out. Little did I know that yesterday was my last hunt. It was over for me. I would never wrestle with voidition again in the way I had for seven years.

I drifted again into the amazing recognition of how long the heart can survive being imprisoned, tortured, drop by drop, out of life. The created somehow lived on hope though they couldn't escape any more than they could crawl out of the creatures. We stay alive in hope as the heartbeat slowly ebbs away into parasympathetic death—not heart, just nervous system survival, even as the creatures buck and jerk for one more drop of the heart and kill in doing it, the way a dead snake can poison with its last instinctive twitch; a grotesque symbiotic mockery of everything that was once human.

I recalled a paragraph, completely forgetting that Josh was awake before me. Ortega y Gasset said, "Man is what happened to him and what he hath done." He spoke of human centaurs, the natural and the extranatural. The natural requires the exertion with the energy of creativity. It does what it does. Creativity does not become thought, though. The extranatural, however, requires a push up against inertia, a decision, daily resolved to live, though we never pull away from the natural; bound as a centaur who can transcend biology through creativity and acceptance that uses biology in a submitted form. I had paraphrased Ortega's thought into my own; heart must take precedence over everything and biology is made to submit for a season, unless we exhaust our hearts in utter isolation and the eye finally goes dark before its time.

I felt my hand squeezed, and looked to see Josh's hand on mine, calling me to him. He must have seen my smile fade as the loss, the violence, the sadness, the rescues and anger all blended into this point in life, and that was only yesterday. Tears had gathered in his eyes and spilled down the sides of the skin stretched over his skull, so sunken were his cheeks. His chin shook slightly and more tears came. I placed my palm under his and held his weak embrace.

I said very quietly so as not to awaken Rachel, "Did I

hurt you, Josh?"

He shook his head slightly and whispered, "No." Tears of relief washed down my cheeks as I spoke. He weakly cleared his throat, and said, "Abe, I'm sorry," with a breath that came from a deep place. I looked at him nonplussed. His voice became a little stronger as he meted out as much story as he could. I urged him to wait until he was stronger to talk, but he shook me off. He slowly talked about how much sorrow each set of eyes carried in the tunnels. He whispered hoarsely that the creatures that still have eyes scramble all the time for places in the underworld to be alone. It means staying alive longer. The greatest danger is the roots that have to be clawed and chewed to continue survival, because that is where we slash each other to our ends and find the insane relief of death.

"To eat is to die; to not eat is to die," he said. The most dangerous creatures have no eyes. They smell and kill; the ones with eyes can avoid death through isolation and trying to avoid the roots, which cannot be done. It's all instinct; all of it. But the eyes still see and remain connected to the heart, witnessing horror after horror while being a part of it in complete helplessness. He then quietly said, "I never would have made it to the opening. I was just looking to eat. My eyes were going out. I couldn't care anymore." He looked sadly at me as he finished with one more statement. "And I would have killed you if I could have, Abe," he whispered finally exhausted again. Tears came to his eyes again, and rolled down his face, just as my tears wet his hand that I had been holding against my face, knowing that I would have killed him first.

I do not believe he heard me whisper, "Josh, I'm sorry. I'm sorry, Josh," as I hugged his hand gently and cried. They all had courage until the last light went out.

XVIII

On the third night after meeting William Williams, who I would meet at midnight, the third full day of Josh's recovery, and the last night of Rachel's stay, the four of us sat at the table to eat. Josh was recovering quickly, considering how close to death he had come. Rachel and Josh both sat at the table and cried while they ate slowly. The gratitude and loss overwhelmed all the convalescing at first. The simplicity of a spoon in one's own hand, sitting at a table with others who care, even being able to walk unassisted to the table was often overwhelming. We would sit, almost meditatively, talk slowly and always let the meal unfold. Sometimes, they would just sit and weep, not able yet to touch the food, frightened of trusting it would come again.

When one of the new people was aroused to talk, the story of will, seduction, and denial unfolded, followed by heavy remorse. Every created had lusted after invincibility over life or become unaffected by life. To avoid inner pain, they refused to attend to the inner voice of their emotional and spiritual makeup. It had taken centuries to dismantle predesign; now the results rushed toward grotesque conclusions. What was once a way of thinking that could be hidden had become substantive. The actions that promoted invincibility, translated safety, slowly evolved into transudation mutation. The inside world that was concealed had become evident and only the inside world being brought outside salved the life of a person.

Not one person we had rescued desired to become isolated. They all craved life, but they didn't want to have to feel it, and the teachers of life had been educated into unbelief, marginalized into being ignored, or had compromised their own awareness to be to be able to discount what they knew. They could be purchased as I had been. The craving for life became the lust for control. They couldn't stop it because they let no one know about it, and the ones who once knew were no longer teaching truth. I remained awed by how the paragraphs had forever spoken of these days, and without them we had no legacy nor did they, no bearing.

Josh and Rachel talked to each other. They also looked at each other with an unspoken recognition of connection. Two emaciated createds looking past the appearance into the possibilities. I knew Rachel and Josh would be OK. Rachel asked Josh if he missed the tunnels at all. Josh dropped his spoon and looked at her abruptly. He then stared, and said, "Yes." I waited to hear what would come next.

Rachel said, "There I knew no future existed, so I didn't have to care; that is the great seduction. I'm still scared to care, to hope even."

I made no comment, as Josh said, "Thank you," to Rachel. Beatrice and I looked at each other; she signaled for me to help her clean up, leaving Rachel and Josh to practice being human again and practice saying goodbye. I was continuing to discover that it would take a lifetime.

Soon after Rachel had departed and Josh slept soundly, Beatrice and I sat in candlelight looking at the map to Williams' place. The moon would be full so I would be able to see more easily; I figured he had planned as much. As eleven drew near, we walked to the cleansing area for me to dress. I felt naked without the dagger. I left the helmet, too, wearing only the tunic, pants and boots. I had not been in the dark away from home without a weapon since the night at the emergency room seven years ago. I was scared. So was Beatrice. William had said that I wouldn't need it. The time had passed, he had said, and I would just have to trust him.

My leather tunic seemed heavy and the canvas pants stiffer. I hugged Beatrice in the moonlight. Touch was never casual; we had learned the sacred act of love was always intertwined with pain. I left her with one look back. We waved, and then I started my run into my uncharted territory, feeling the night's air on my whole face for the first time in years.

After two miles, according to the map, I began an ascent up a half-mile rise where I would turn sharply on a cutback and head into Ebenezer Valley. When I reached the top to turn down to the valley, I stopped, startled by immensity. Where I stood on the cap of my climb on a dead end of land seemed one step from entering the stars. The vastness of the sky startled the breath from me, and all I could breathe back in was awe and gratitude. Star upon star, the full moon behind me, the Milky Way like a blanket of light more than separate stars spread out endlessly. I suddenly felt my smallness and yet instead of becoming a speck, I saw how much what I do matters, how I'm made to live matters, so I can be a part of all of this life, no matter how cold it seems. I gave this moment no philological underpinning, no historical connection, no paragraph, no reference point, but my own heart swelled with life's yearning to live. I laughed at how simple it all became in that moment. I am not big; but I am a big deal. I had always run from such simplicity. I could miss my life by letting small mean nothing or not big mean everything. I decided to eat forever from the banquet table of the child from then on, no matter the end.

Like a cliché of disbelief, a shooting star crossed the sky in a second. I followed its trail and headed towards the valley. Within a mile I could see a light about another mile away. Like William had drawn, four and four-tenths miles from my door to his. I assumed with a picture of him in my mind that he was being exact. I began another descent after a cutback and was within a quarter mile of the place. A huge barn, more like warehouse, loomed before me; no house. I started walking in, staring at the place when suddenly a blinding light flashed at my feet and in my face, and the sound of growling dogs rushing towards me shocked me into a terrified crouch as I grabbed for the dagger that wasn't there. A voice over a loudspeaker garbled a warning, demanding that I stop where I stood and identify myself or suffer the consequences. I shielded my eyes for the attack and screamed my name, "It's Abe! Abe! You fool!"

Then I heard laughter coming over the loudspeaker, "Hee, hee, hee," as I heard the loud click of the speaker go off as the light went out. I still couldn't see, and I really wanted to get to Williams very fast so I could damage him quickly. He had stepped out the door and moved towards me; I could smell him before my eyes could adjust to catch him and take him to the ground. I found his outline. "What do you think about that?" he was saying. "No dogs either. It's an automatic warning system. All prerecorded." I yelled at him to put the megaphone down before I made him eat it.

"I live a scared man's life," he squalled. "Thought you'd really be impressed. Hadn't had a chance to use it yet. You're the first intruder...well, you know what I mean."

"I'm duly impressed, William," very slowly settling into a normal breathing rhythm, already wondering if my hope for more and need to have a friend in mission was making me the fool again. I was also glad I had not brought my dagger. He turned the megaphone off as it made a scratchy shrill squeal before closing. Chuckling uneasily, minimally grasping the impact of what he had just done, he raised his arms in welcome and then gave me a bear hug as if we had known each other forever. I was shocked again as he turned towards the barn and said excitedly with arms outstretched, "Come on, we have to eat and then there's lots to do, Dr. Philology. Come on in to my warehouse, doctor's office, library, laboratory, factory, and home, all under one roof! Come on in!" he beckoned as he slid the heavy door open with a grunt. "I have tea steeping. My own brew. Papa taught me some of it. Warm you up and calm you down."

I stepped into the well-lit place and could hardly believe the scene as I heard the door slide behind me and click safely into place. In front of me, some 30 feet away a fire blazed, a bear rug in front of it, head pointed our way in a growl. Two giant leather chairs sat to each side of the hearth. The floor of the whole place was laid with large sheets of what appeared to be granite, gray as storm clouds and rough-cut. Every six feet or so were lanterns, turned up to full light around the walls. To my right, bookshelves, floor to about 12 feet above and extending at least another 30 feet were full of volumes, with no space for anymore. Above the shelves hung logging chains, maps, animal traps, and what else I couldn't see yet.

William hollered from the other end of the warehouse for me to make myself at home while he finished up the feast. I didn't even turn to his voice, even when I heard hissing of some sort of device coming from his direction. I didn't want to miss anything before me. A long butcher-block sawmill grade pine table that sat in front of the shelves was covered with books. A lamp at each end standing at least four feet above the table shined brightly down on the books. Green bankers' shades covered the lights, and wings of brass extended out from the stands as if angels were looking down at the table. I walked towards the table. Volumes of twos and threes were covering the table, some open face up, others with their spines facing me. Science and philosophy, medicine, psychology, history, art, architecture and engineering. Drawings of bridges and diagrams of movable, rolling buildings and bridges, catapults and metal refining covered the walls and other tables and counter tops opposite the reading table and beyond the bookshelves. At the sidewall were pictures and diagrams of cantilevers and water turbine works, tunnel digging plans, even handwritten lists of historical escapes, and atrocities like Masada and Auschwitz.

A yellowed copy of *The Serenity Prayer* by Neibuhr hung crookedly in the middle of wall pinnings. A large framed copy of *The Declaration of Independence* hung nearby as I looked to my left. Someone, I guessed William, had relabeled it, *The Declaration of Dependence*. I turned to my left and William was standing nearby observing what I was observing, quiet as air. He said that he would explain that title some time, because if anyone reads the first paragraph, it is very clearly a statement of dependence upon how we are created for liberty from tyranny. We declared independence from tyranny, not from how we are created or what we are created to be like. It all fit; I knew the paragraph well.

He pointed to the table. I told him that I would be right there as I walked slowly along the walls toward the eating table. Cinching up his pants and pushing up his glasses, he told me to take my time and he walked slowly with me, without saying a word. The place spoke and yet had to be deciphered. The inner person was displayed in all of its creative chaos everywhere. An open scroll of *Desideratum* was unrolled on a table, a nail punch at each end holding it open. Another scroll of wise sayings was nailed to a roof support post. Paintings were hung everywhere, Old Masters, Hudson School, a Picasso plate, Dade, drawings of Da Vinci, play bills up to the 1960s, which mystified me, to which William just shrugged his shoulders. Photographs of Artist Point in Yellowstone, Amazonian bows and arrows, a suit of armor leaned against a post.

I did not know if I stood in a museum, a factory, or a cathedral when I saw above my head a plastered section of the ceiling that had Michelangelo's painting of the *Creation of Man*, signed by William and dated two years previously. Below the painting he had written the Latin phrase, *sacrosanctus reverentia*, in sacred worship. All he said was, "I painted it to feel it, to feel it as completely as I could, to absorb it if I could, to make what it said mine, the way the creatures make others' theirs. You see, the Creator moves out of a heart's ventricle, don't you?" Indeed I had seen it, but had never talked to anyone but Beatrice about it.

Then he said kindly, "Let's eat. We will have a long night ahead, and I'm hungry." Those were the first normal words I had ever heard him speak.

IXX

———

To my left a kitchen table was clean but for two place settings and a diffuser in the middle puffing out a scent I did not know until William saw me observing it. "Valor oil," he said, "a mix of six oils thought to allow us to absorb and elicit hidden strengths." I turned to him, still taking it all in, when he pushed up his glasses and shrugged, "every little bit helps." I then saw the pile of books, papers and gadgets that had been stacked to the side to make room for us to eat. I glanced up into the rafters to how he had spanned such a large space with so few posts to support it. I realized that the beams reaching across the span were continuous, at least 40 feet in length and probably 14 by 14 squared. The ingenuity to build this place and the materials acquired had taken rare gifts to attain and implement.

In the loft above the beams I could see lots of planed wood, nets of rope, animal traps, small cages, bags of concrete, mortar and seeds, both of grasses and crops, pulleys and tackle, log snatchers, an acetylene torch and a welder, with a plasma cutter, something I didn't even know still existed. "Built the place years and years ago, with Papa, Mom, and my brothers," William began to explain after seeing me continue to examine everything in wonder. "They are all gone now," he said looking down to the kitchen table, which I realized easily had room for eight people. I assumed around this table many feasts with family and friends had occurred. "Pulleys, fulcrums, angles...they are our answer for now. The cantilever fascinates me now and now is when we need it. We are going to build one," matter-of-factly stated as if I were up to date. "The supporting structures we will use are all from railroad bridge beams, dropped off in the woods some distance from here years ago when the changeover occurred. Heart of pine, forgotten like the tracks no longer needed." A slight smile came to me at how disarming and pure William seemed to be, yet grieved by scenes that he had not shared.

Amongst all the distinct scents, from tea to kerosene, clove to valor oil, wood burning, grain and hay, the succulent scent of barbeque cut through them all. "Let's eat," William chortled and turned toward a cooker large enough to smoke seven roasts at once. "Smoked it earlier, seven hours of perfection. Tea and meat, with my own sauce. Make the sauce over there," he said pointing to an area near the table, loaded with measuring devices, goggles and the elemental chart on a board. I also noticed a catalogue of the language of flowers from the 1800s. "The clove," he said as he put the platter of smoking meat on the table, "is from Madagascar, no purer clove on earth. Hard to acquire it now."

He reached back to the kitchen space and brought a large bowl of dark, thick sauce to the table, with a ladle in the bowl. "Abe, everything that carries DNA has an energy fingerprint," stated with the same tone of voice that he spoke of barbeque. He spoke of everything with a sense of wonder and matter-of-factness. "Life pulses with it as you know and have written," he said looking straight at me through glasses that had a film on them from the cooker. I had not thought of having written in years, and was struck by William's reference to being familiar with my writing. Before I could think further, he continued. "It has a sound, even a backbeat like the humming of a million, trillion beehives or the echoing sound of thundering horses galloping across a plain with caves below amplifying the sound. We listen only to what we hear, not to all that is true. If we stimulate cells within the context of creation, life itself, outside of us, takes on the enhancement that has blessed our lives beyond imagination. But when we reduce ourselves to biology or genetics only, the electricity of our concentration reduces life to materialism only. We reduce life to a whimper or a silence that becomes deafening to people who cannot shut off.

The createds we have rescued and the ones who will never be rescued couldn't turn it off any more than we can, and their need to silence it overruled their core with the grotesque results that were always true but not clearly seen until the inverse of biology and the essential of a person collided with bizarre material results. The Collective itself is aptly

named because of the 'collective' unspoken contract to exist
in denial, real denial that means blind and deaf to an inner
self, the nether land results of the agenda to avoid humanity
for humanity's good. It has happened for centuries. Think
Stalin. All we can do is stare in disbelief or move on. Do you
know that Collective thinks of us, the 'lost people' they call
us, as being blind and deaf to what we cannot see, unreason-
able and genetically deficient. In them we see part of Archimedes' principle tragically fulfilled. A ball of air can be forever suspended if pushed under water deeply enough to have
no pressure to rise. Perfectly balanced. Eternally suspended.
Nothing. But denial has to remain entrenched to survive. All
agendas have to maintain the status quo of denial.

That could have been our end were it not for the great
good fortune of this war of love," he chuckled as he ended,
speaking profoundly while busied with domestic chores,
some time after midnight this night. He sliced into the lamb
shoulder, releasing more heat and aroma into the area that
conjured in me every memory of what feast was meant to
be. He sat, motioning me to join as he cinched up his pants
again before sitting in a large rough-hewn armed chair with
a tall ladder-back. He stopped for a moment after sitting;
while still looking at the table, he said, "Abe, I am thankful
for you, my friend, and for the bounty of this meal; I am
thankful for life and I bow to the One who made us so able
to wonder and have such joy, sadness and love." He left his
head down in silence for a moment, then looked up, push-

ing his glasses at the same time, smiled and said, "Let's eat. Tell me if you love this sauce," he said as he poured a ladle full over the smoking meat on his plate. It had the thickness of warm honey, yet the scent of peppers, ginger, and brown sugars. "Papa and Mom's recipe. The honey is from here.

As I was saying," he went on among bites and big swigs of warm tea, as I did the same, simply amazed at the taste of the lamb, the sauce and the cleansing taste of the tea. I had at first thought the meal too sparse.

"Archimedes saw beyond science, which didn't even exist at the time. He saw himself as a philosopher. He saw and wondered about life and living. No separation and compartmentalization had been falsely formed. Newton, the same," he said as he refilled my thick glass cup and his own with tea. The aromas, including the diffuser, the place, the time of night, all heightened my senses and my joy. "Newton wrote more words concerning the mysteries and profound sacred in the ancient Scripture than he did about his discoveries of natural law. Over a million words, privately stored away, not discovered until long after his death. His concern was mystery, the desire to live in it more than to contain it or codify it." All of these words were familiar to me, having written about and followed a wide range of pursuits. But what Williams said next reawakened me to a world I had pursued little in depth since leaving the Collective years ago.

"Listen to what Newton said about what appears to be a simple passage from the prophet Isaiah, himself a man of detail about mystery. Isaiah said:

> *'Let him who walks in the dark,*
> *who has no light,*
> *trust in the name of the LORD*
> *and rely on his God.*
> *But now, all you who light fires*
> *and provide yourselves with flaming torches*
> *go, walk in the light of your fires*
> *and of the torches you have set ablaze.*
> *This is what you shall receive from my hand:*
> *You will lie down in torment.'*

Isaiah took that material and saw the surrender to the process of Presence, a good relational Presence that offers life, if we catch the flow of life. The torment is created by rejection of the offer in the mystery. We ourselves establish the torment—not life. We equate mystery with drowning and destroy ourselves in the clutching after that which will do no more than torment us with hatred toward mystery. When we 'light our own torches,' we move away from the personal DNA fingerprint of how we are made, we leave behind a greater desire than survival; we miss our lives fulfillment. Our lives become controlled by myopia; for the sake of control, we lose being known. Life is in the mystery more than the material.

Democritus guessed well with atoms; Lucretius made

it sound beautiful, as you know," William looked at me, assuming my background. I wondered where he was headed, for all of these things were familiar to me though we had never spoken of them, and certainly no one had identified the research that identified Lucretius' use of poetic beauty, the language of mystery to discard mystery and make meaning an illusion and death with it. To my knowledge only Dr. Narahoshi and I had ever spoken of such, and I dimly remembered that I had not read that section of the paper at the last conference where I presented.

Lucretius had made meaninglessness in mystery an art form. He had helped turn that which we could not see into non-existence and the mystery of what we did not know into emptiness. Hope could not be seen; longings could not be seen. I realized William was still talking among bites, while I was recalling how familiar what he spoke about was to me. He had just said, "Darkness, despair, destruction and death," when he came fully into focus and I saw that he was smiling at me, both hands palm down on the table. Those words were an addition to everything I had known. The war of love had been going on for several thousand years now. Milton had been one of its advocates in light, hope, creation and courage.

He looked quizzically at me as he continued, like he was about to tell the conclusion to a great joke, but instead he continued with words that had meta-meaning in voice inflection and facial movement. "We have moved to a time that goes as follows: spiritual evolution increases speed in which the molecular movement of mystery is being made material and silence has a voice. The backbeat is becoming deafening. Reverse transudation is just one example with its reptilian results. The members of the Collective also become removed from life, but they have for the most part defeated humanity and are as removed as a computer from the DNA of creation, their own form of superseding biology. They have no anguish from what I can tell," he said with certainty. "Biology is the cherished material possession and the Collective is even removed from that these days," he said reaching for a swig of tea to finish his meal.

The meat was gone, the platter picked clean; a glass of tea remained for each of us. I felt full and alive, and still deeply tired. So much of what he said to me was so familiar that a couple of times I could easily have finished William's thoughts. "The only hope for the createds is rebirth and what a grotesque womb, aye," he said with a sigh that carried years of work, thought, experience, dreams and prayer. I knew that sigh. As he pushed back from the table and rose, he said, "Let's finish our drinks by the fire; something else you need to know. We will be departing here at 2:30. We have a great task to complete, for let me say referring to the great Milton, that the Adamantine chains have been broken, but for nature's own the robins will sing and the frog's croak again," as he looked directly at me as we moved to the fire.

"Those words are mine, drawn from a scene one spring

on our place. They are from the paper at the conference, words I did not read, nor would I have wasted that precious reference on the Collective." I said staring back at him.

William stopped to look back. "Abe," he said, "you are quite well-known and neither you nor Beatrice actually know it. Many of the words I share with you this night are enlightened by the last paper you ever wrote, the one you didn't finish and left at the conference."

I sat down in a large leather chair stunned by what I heard. William sat, too, as he continued. "Dr. Narahashi saw you leave the conference. She saw you leave the paper and your jacket. She understood what you were doing. Two days later she did the same. That night, she picked up your paper, but left your jacket," he said smiling. "She took it east, back home. She left copies here and the words in it have spread all over the world. They have become a treatise on our purpose, and an understanding of our passion. That paper is part of an underground movement of regional freedoms all over the earth. Your sons are very familiar with it and are quite proud of you. Doctor has taken it and taught it everywhere he goes. All by mail and face-to-face relationship, gatherings of people all over looking for life in life. Dr. Narohashi has become one of the great hunters and teachers in the underground. "Your past is no waste, dear friend." William leaned back in his chair with a piercing look towards me as I turned towards the fire with tears in my eyes as I remembered what my sons said to me about not being alone. I had no idea. The knowledge, indeed, had great use.

"One other thing, which might help you grasp how much I know," William said somberly, still looking at me with a sad and grave look. "A woman you know who is one of the grand movers in the Collective is a Dr. Sybil Williams," he started. Again, more pieces fell into place to let me see the width and breadth of our work. I remembered the look on her face as I walked from the conference. She sat on the end of an aisle, and did not acknowledge me when I left the dais. She reminded me of a Gila monster. I remembered my fear from that night.

"I was married to Sybil. She left me years ago. I tried to warn her over and over; she became more convinced with my every attempt that I was insane at worst, stuck in the provincialism of my people and puerile at best. The more she became convinced that hope had essentially become antiquated as an experience that had to be associated with pain, the more removed she became from the person I had always known. We grew up together in this valley, Abe. The Collective, however, early on also recognized our cognitive capacities. My Papa never trusted them. She didn't have people that valued her. The last time I saw her was right here. I told her that I would never stop loving her, but could not cut out my heart to stay with her. She stood quickly and slapped me as hard as she could on her way out the door. I sat in this very chair for a day after she left. I have written her many times, but never heard from her again," he whispered as his voice trailed off into the memory of the last time he had seen the person who had been as much a part of William as the valley itself.

William picked up his flute, after offering me a Costa Rican cigar. Before he began to play, he said, "You brought all the pearls we needed to awaken peacemakers everywhere. Your paper also showed the thread that connects the pearls to draw a post-cultural humanity back to its roots." William stared at the fire for a bit in silence and then began to play quietly for himself. I watched the fire, listening to the flute and crackling embers. I heard an owl screech somewhere nearby as I sat in the wonder of it all. I missed Beatrice and our sons. I rested in the stillness.

XX

William played plaintively as the embers of the fire and my cigar died down. He finished what was the last quiet note. While still holding the flute in his lap with both hands, he said, "My Papa drew me to the reality that the sciences were a tool we could exult in beautifully, but one that was always to be submitted to the truth, as an enrichment of this life." He shifted in his chair to look at me. "Papa schooled us in the sciences and everything about you here speaks to the use of the tools, but he kept the wonder. His grandfather wrote *The Language of Flowers* you saw and we have never departed from the language. I miss Papa awfully, the way you miss your sons, your people, and have missed your brother. He is in my heart like a flame and in my being like oxygen."

"Our missings," I said, "like you with your Papa, I now know reside within us as our greatest gifts. To have known love like we have, even in the pain of it, validates the existence we have in the fullness of our lives now. The heart of who we are is made for such love and, therefore, trouble and pain. I have learned this truth over and over again in the paragraphs, certainly. Even more, the paragraphs do no more than speak to that which is in us all. The unprovable heart I know is either lived or missed in that gap," pointing up towards the Creation painting and the space between the fingers that almost touch. "Either it links us or we remain forever lost in an abandoned life," I finished as I looked towards William.

William looked at me in a way that reminded me of a golden retriever that glances over at someone it trusts without moving its head. He said sort of talking out of the side of his mouth as if someone else could hear us talking, "I'm going to tell you something you may think makes me sound weird." I looked at him at first attempting to hide my wonderment at the absurdity of his statement. I held my breath for a moment, and then couldn't help but burst out laughing from my gut. He looked at me confused and watched me laughing, nonplussed, which made me laugh even harder as I leaned forward. Then he chuckled.

I tried to say, "Me think you're crazy? No!" with faux surprise, but was laughing too hard at the irony of even that. William began to laugh, too, when I spread my arms out, then stood to point my hands at all that surrounded us in this warehouse-cathedral-laboratory-home. I said almost as if from a stage projecting into the back row of the auditorium, "We sit in leather chairs with our boots on a bear rug, with a head frozen in a growl, staring into the dark, at 2:00 in the morning after seven years of the insane, inexplicable, and the impossible being sane, understandable, and possible, rescuing createds, and now we plan some mission that I don't grasp, but remain willing to stay in no matter what, with a person I just met seventy-two hours ago! Why would I think you strange, and why would I think me sane?"

He got it and began to laugh hard, pushing up his glasses as he stood and bent over laughing so hard he had to remove his glasses to wipe his eyes and his glasses, which I noted finally cleaned the smoke from the cooker. He said something about being able to see, not even realizing he had been looking through a fog in his glasses for hours, which made us laugh even more.

I then mockingly said, "You smell like a spice factory and kerosene refinery, and you just finished a tune on your bamboo flute that you handmade somewhere in this place. And you haven't changed clothes in no telling how long. I'm wearing a double-layered leather tunic that has been covered with more goop than I can barely consider, that is usually paired with a leather helmet! I think every single thing about us is weird. So," I said slowly so that he would understand clearly, taking a breath and slowing down from laughing, "I think I will not think you crazy," I concluded. "Peculiar we are and free men, made so by heart's passion and perseverance in a vision. My friend, you and I are positively peculiar," I said to finish talking as I waited to hear what William would share.

He bent over and put his hands on his knees to take a breath. As he rose up, he said, "Abe, I'll tell you what I was going to say anyway," with a short chuckle. "And it is a prejudice of taste yet connected to the thread we spoke of earlier." I recollected the pearls and thread comments he had made. He went on, "An old song written what seems like a thousand years ago was inspired by what I believe was the last American play to have merit, the end of the thread in stage drama. It brought the hero of romantic meaning to life again—*The Man from La Mancha*—the life of Don Quixote living in a world that had lost its way.

To Dream the Impossible Dream is the song. It speaks of our lives, the passion and the purpose, I mean really. We look crazy, but I tell you that song never leaves me. It speaks to me still, the life progression, the courage to stay in all the phases of life from awakening to the end. If I die over the next few days, will you please make sure that anthem for my life is played in the same manner I play the flute. I believe in the words, and I have lived them. They speak to the truth of the hero's life, which I have lived, and so have you and Beatrice and your sons." I looked at him, a little stunned. It was true, yet I had been too falsely humble to admit it. We don't ever stop hiding from the truth.

"The song ties a knot in the thread to hold all the pearls. The truth ended back there. No other song has equaled it since," William said and then ended with, "I'm with Sophocles. Better to die with honor than live without it." He looked at me with great earnestness, staring, and I said that I would do as he asked.

"You don't think I'm being too sentimental?" he asked like a child asking if I thought the wind would become a tornado. I told him that I remembered the song, and that the words of hope in the song could only be considered sentimental by a coward. "Good," William said, with a return from his fear, and then, "we better move on. Two miles south of here is our destination." He cinched his pants up as he turned to head out. I followed without any questions. I trusted William Williams. I trusted every move we had been making for years.

As he slid the door shut, I remembered working with a rock mason in my teens. He had a tattoo of a skull and crossbones on his left shoulder that stretched down onto his biceps, a black beard and black eyes like a raven's. He spoke in a gravelly voice, when he spoke, which was seldom. I hauled the stone, mixed much of the mortar, which he used sparingly because the focus of his work was to make each rock fit like a puzzle piece giving the sense that every wall, chimney or arch he made looked like dry stack. He chiseled into shape every piece of the puzzle and then found where it fit to create his mosaic. He didn't know where the wall or chimney would take him until he was finished.

One mid-morning I had finished hauling limestone rocks into a pile that he would pull from to build a rock wall in a house. The wall was 14 feet high and 21 feet wide. I remember one time he put down his rock chisel and sat staring at the wall. He had laid only four stones all morning. He stared and stared. I didn't ask anything. I waited. I finally sat, too, on the pile of rocks I hauled in. Finally, he said aloud to no one I thought, "The rocks aren't talking to me." He paused, then stood, and ended his day with me by saying, "the man upstairs picks them out." He then left, saying something about seeing me in the morning. I couldn't understand how he could ever finish a wall four stones at a time. I wasn't sure he was the right fellow to work with, but I continued and so did the wall. He finished and our conversations were sparse, beyond me watching and supplying him with stone. I remember the hauling days from old rock fences we found in the country or the hottest days down in the old quarry that had a thousand years' worth of stone to haul out. I became very strong during that time, and quieter, more able to wait to see.

When the wall was finished, I began to collect tools and prepare to sweep the site. He stopped me and told me to come to the wall to see. He then took me on a tour of the stones. So clearly I remember his voice as he said some day a child would come along and trace in the two indentations of one stone with their fingers that could seem like rivers in the stone. Then he showed me where a slight crack had been left at the bottom to the left of a stone that gave the appearance of not being joined well, which I knew he had to have intended. He asked me to look in the opening and see the quartz "cat-eye" in the stone that reflects the light. He showed me more of the wall, and ended with "everything shows a story, even things that don't know that they even exist." After that summer ended and I went back to school, I never saw him again.

XXI

T he night air filled my lungs as we trekked south, up and over several rises, through thickets and twisting cutbacks. We walked in silence for some time. I hunted this time of night and was content to move in silence, though I wanted to know where we were headed and for what.

"Abe," William said, stopping as if I had spoken, "we are headed to what we call the hive, to the place the last years have brought us to." He then turned and began walking again. Then he went on to explain our purpose, as much as I could gather through words rather than experience. He said that we were going down into a concrete channel, one that acts as a path for several million gallons of decontaminated wastewater that the energy plant dumps at planned intervals before dawn light. The Collective has been covering up a lie for years that they have invented a new energy source derived from an electrical-chemical intervention that reacts with the incineration of garbage to create power. Their crown jewel of energy efficiency is a lie. The garbage is incinerated without smoke, done very efficiently, by the way, but the energy is a well-contained use of nuclear power. It lights the whole region. Other areas are still using coal, too, practicing the zero emissions technology that is being used on the garbage. The regions where coal comes from are off limits to the general population because the areas are considered nuclear contamination sites from the past before we were told that we no longer used nuclear energy." He shook his head.

William went on to tell me that the plant produces clean, abundant energy and is a model of our collective abilities, but the Collective will not allow their true efficiency to be noted because it goes against the agenda of control. He stopped abruptly in the dark and I could tell that he was looking at me incredulously before he uttered the word, "Crazy!" with a loud snort. "The belief that the natural laws of the universe can be bypassed rather than cooperated with is implausible and insane. The counter disbelief that the spiritual processes of the universe can likewise be discounted as having no substance is just as absurd, and psychotic. The universe is full of the unknown, the mystery, all substantive, whether we can see it or not. The Collective's attempt to assume that only the material is the spiritual, and the denial of the reality of the spiritual itself has scarred everything. The denial of neediness, not just need, but neediness of our inner design has brought us to such insanity, so off course that we pretend a very real and well-coordinated use of energy is made from something that has not even been invented. Words and their suggestion have become the truth instead of tools that allow us to express imperfectly the mystery of the infinite. Just think of the word coal—it means something that is pejorative at best, a contaminate of humanity, death and evil at worst," he said talking to everyone, himself, me and no one.

He explained that the water exiting from the plant was like a giant flush from a gigantic commode and that the water was as clean as a high mountain spring. It runs from the plant down the channel for one mile into a twenty by twenty culvert drain. The water then drops 45 feet below the earth into an abandoned mine shaft channel. It then travels the other direction almost another mile before cascading a thousand feet into a canyon that leads into a valley beyond it. The description sounded a lot like I remember the waterfall at Artist's Point in the old Yellowstone Park.

But William explained that no one had yet seen the waterfall from the outside. "We can only see it fall, and look out of the eye of the opening into the valley below," he said. "Seventy seven feet exactly from the mouth of our cavern is the cliff side of a plateau, the surface of which is covered with pines and hardwoods, and it runs for miles. It has no human inhabitants from what we can see, and plenty of wildlife. It is a 'no-zone' or site that is said to be uninhabitable because of strip mining, even though the mining companies spent millions of dollars to cooperatively operate within the context of changing the landscape, but not the environment itself. They behaved responsibly. Do you realize we do the same thing when we grow food in a garden? We use the soil, take from the soil and must return nutrients to the soil to restore it so it can continue to feed us. That is solely our responsibility.

The land has been restored, which you know means return home again! We are going to cross that 77 feet and begin again. The time has come. The Collective needs for us to get out of the way or we fear the consequences," he said as he grabbed my shoulder to make his point very clear. "As long as we have moved silently and in the dark we have been ignored, but there are too many of us now to be ignored any-more," William ended with a warning chortle.

We walked up a rise, falling silent again. I heard crickets, which always brought me peace in the night and slight breezes in the limbs of the trees. Our footsteps on the path were the only other sound. I could see the lights of the plant in the distance as I looked downward from the top of the rise. A trail of steam exited the spiraling stacks above the plant, drifting away in the south breeze. The plant was less than a mile away.

William said, "We'll head northwest down towards the channel where the wall of water will hit the metal drain. Halfway there we will cross the old railroad tracks. Note the wooded area where we cross; our work tomorrow will be there." Before I could ask the how, when or what do you mean, he went on to the next topic. "Abe, all those people you have been following all those years in your academic career and then in the readings of the paragraphs, the same ones Papa taught me; they are our brothers and sisters, our very own kin of the heart. Each one of them knew exactly whom they spoke of and searched out. They gave their lives to their attachment—all of them, even poor old Descartes. As you know so well from your research, his work was taken hostage. He tried to prove what we already knew to defend something that needed no defense.

"In an attempt to eradicate bizarre superstition, the control-focused rationalists and scientists also eradicated *sentio ergo sum* instead of allowing this most human condition to be part and parcel of that which drives, even compels, us to search out the mysteries of life. The self was eradicated from the search and minimized into nonexistence. Aquinas quit talking when he realized what was happening. Friedrich Nietzsche railed against them for their theft yet hated being human; Dickens knew, Cowper, Donne, Marlowe and Goethe and Erasmus before them knew. John Newton, who penned the greatest anthem of all time to life's rebirth, he knew. So did Cervantes, who mourned the loss, and Miguel de Unamuno, Marcel, and Ortega, who could not get over the mystery of our hope. That is how come I love *The Impossible Dream* so much. It is the summary of how we live if we know.

"Heck, Abe, I even love Jiminy Cricket." I laughed aloud in spite of the seriousness of every word William spoke and the integrations he made. "Walt Disney, you remember him?" William went on.

I stopped to say, "Yes." And there we stood in open

ground talking about *The Impossible Dream*, Walt Disney, Jiminy Cricket.

He said, "Walt Disney created Jiminy Cricket so that Pinocchio could understand himself and become more than just a thing that existed. He would be a real boy, but he needed a voice that could speak to how he was created to be. Remember, you came alive again when you remembered how you were made. You and Bea found each other again. I came back to life, too, even in my sorrow of losing Sybil. You were reborn the minute you walked out of the conference. Your fear was even part of the life that drove you to leave, not having a clue where you were headed but for home. That's what we are all doing. And that is what the next two or three days will be about. Even the lilies know it, Abe. The lilies and Sir Isaac Newton. Humph," William grunted loudly and stared intensely towards me. He then bear hugged me tightly.

I feared for my own sanity because I understood and was moved by every word he spoke.

XXII

———

We arrived at the grate, lit dimly by the lights from the plant in the distance. The bottom of the concrete channel was dry and slanted up on the sides at least 25 feet on each side. The width of the floor and the grate were the same, 20 feet exactly, William told me. The grate was one inch thick metal with six by six inch square holes that let water through. He looked at his watch that glowed in the dark when he pushed the adjuster, like one I had as a child. William saw that I noticed and was smiling. "Papa gave it to me. Takes a lickin' and keeps on tickin'," he snickered. "It's 3:27. In three minutes the gates will open. You will hear the roar of thunder that is the water rushing towards us. Your waiting and hoping will end here at the drain. Better hang on to your ying yang, get it, yin and yang," he laughed what I thought was too loud as he laid his back against the drain and indeed crossed his hands in front of him, across his crotch.

I did likewise, and just as I settled against the grate, I looked up to see the thunder of a wall of water cascading towards us with a roar that froze me. The last thing I heard was William shouting, "Make like mercury," as he looked straight into my face and eyes with a blissful smile.

"The Roman god of messages!" I screamed in confused terror.

"No, the thermometer!" he screamed back as we lost each other in the sudden crush of a wall of water that slammed me into the grate and knocked the wind out of me. I immediately began to suffocate, crushed, unable to cry out with the giant hand of water controlling everything but my heart's desire to live. I thought of Beatrice, my insanity to be drowning like this, my sons, my brother, the createds. What had William done? What mistake had he made? He was insane.

I was dying, conscious, and covered in blackness. I yielded myself; I remembered the prayers of the child. Darkness covered me completely. Then I saw myself floating, bowed down in prayer by the windows in my own home. The warmth of the dawning sun had just reached the windows. I love; do with me what you will; I have hoped and waited. The last breath left me as the battle of the blanket of water and darkness took me. I began to melt, to separate and slide, rushing away, ushering through; my desire to love turned into a million drops scattered everywhere, falling and identified by the love of me, surrendered and gone. I disappeared, and went with the water, floating on the tops of drops downward, washed pure, falling in pieces, each one a drink, a million drinks to roots, dirt, movements of cells combining, reaching up pushing through the soil, stretching out to the sun, leaves unfurling, extending their fingers with vein pulsing life to absorb and exhale, rolling over clouds. Then it all stopped.

Stillness, silence, breath, longing and contentment finding a home resting in a clean pool of water of millions and millions of drops.

Then suddenly my head snapped upwards as I drew a deep instinctive gasp of air, followed by choking and spitting. I heard a voice as from a great distance shouting, "My glasses! My glasses! Dagnabit! I always forget to put them in my pocket!" I began to focus slowly, knowing that voice anywhere. The distant voice was within two feet of my face. William was thrashing around in the water with his hands feeling for his glasses on the bottom. I blinked several times and gasped again. My rib cage ached and lungs burned. "There you are," William said, raising his glasses into the air triumphantly. He put them on and looked at me through the rivulets that ran down the lenses, making his eyes seem even bigger than normal.

"See, Abe, like mercury, the thermometer," William squeaked delighted, amidst his own gasps for air. He stood up now knee deep in the water. "We become like mercury, a very minute trace mineral in us, you know. Turns out, it has very useful purposes we never knew about until the advancements threw us forward. In surrender, it assists us in spreading out everywhere and yet we never lose our identities if we have one, one that is from within. I wanted you to know how much you have. You are most courageous and whole, Abe. You have been coming to this all of your life. Your *telos* comes from the depth of your surrender." All I knew for sure at the moment was that I was alive, sitting in a pool of water wondering really if perhaps I might just be dreaming, when William pulled up his soaking wet pants, like normal, as if nothing in particular had just happened. He then turned, walked out of the pool and sloshed up a set of steps carved into the stone that I just began to recognize.

I shook my head to clear it more, opened and shut my eyes several times to attempt to focus. As I began to gather my senses, I looked upwards at the rock walls that rose stories above me. The walls had openings up and down and as far down the channel as I could see. I could barely take in the magnificence of what I saw even though I had just been separated into millions of drops and reconciled. The walls had verandas, and steps, fountains that allowed water to run in rivulets down the carved patterns in the stone. A soft reflective light seemed to come from the ceiling above, 45 feet above, I now remembered William had said that's what the drop would be. I opened and shut my eyes again to make sure. Still the same scene. The pool I realized was a holding tank of sorts, like an eddy behind the waterfall that had hit and run down the river channel away from where I sat. The channel was now empty of water except for the light shimmer of evidence that it had just been there. I had entered a place in which great thought and grand action had combined to build this place.

Then, I recognized a murmur. Voices, faces, smiling expectantly at me, a joy expressed in the voices. The people were of all mature ages, fresh and alive like open blooms of flowers. Createds, all of them. This place was the transfer site. Several of them reached towards me to lift me up from the water. They hugged me and then others who were around them began to hug me and pat me on the shoulders and back, smiling and welcoming me like a pet that had disappeared and suddenly returned home. I hugged them back weakly and clumsily as I shifted from the impact of landing moments before, to the impact of who these people were. I knew their faces, but they were now so alive. We all began to walk forward, the circle of createds opening up to reveal the magnificence of my first real sight of the hive. No words could fully describe the industry and artistry of the place.

And there were children, lots of children, though I would not find out this trip whose they were. This reality of great sadness had ached inside me since the hunting began. I never rescued children, which made sense, but I wondered where they went. I would find out later that most of the children were lost to the Collective, another cost of the creatures' control of the createds' lives. The children I saw had been rediscovered, cared for by those people in the region who had stayed the course of remaining free. Still others were simply gone.

William, I vaguely recalled, said something about

catching up later. The hive, or beehive, I assumed meant activity. The place was active, certainly, like a city coming to life in the morning. Createds up and down the length of the channel, and I could see darkness at the end of the river channel that was the opening William had mentioned. They moved about, walking and conversing, working at tasks that seemed part of the routine, like preparing for the day of business. A hum of movement, purposeful, participating in a direction, more like preparing as on a dock before a ship sails. I could hear the echo of rock hammers and compressors coming from the end of the channel. I thought of bees that move with a passion, a purpose, and a plan, but their flight patterns look like joyful, even chaotic meandering.

I stood still. Cliff balconies rose stories above me, ferns grew over the sides of the landings, and geraniums, petunias, and ivies hung in baskets over the edges of the balconies. The water rivulets that were channeled down the cliff edges gathered in pools and then spilled over to the next. They were watering stations for drinking and watering plants. The sound of the water created a certain calm in the midst of the bustling activity. Moss grew in places along the walls. Doors were cut into the walls, just like in a hive, except they were entrances to homes, I soon discovered.

A memory dawned on me of a place Beatrice and I had explored for a week, the quarried marble roads, ancient columns rising along a thoroughfare that suggested glory then faded. Ancient Ephesus returned to life along the main road that led to the library and amphitheater that held 20,000 spectators. But this "Ephesus" was expanded beyond belief.

I turned to my guides and smiled in wonder at the first created I had carried on my back some seven years ago. We hugged in delight, and then I saw two more people I had carried into re-creation, a woman and another man, one twenty and the other about fifty. We hugged like a reunion after years and years.

They began to tell me of their temporary city, their dwellings, courtyards within them, use of water flow, how they had developed solar lighting with mirrors that could be adjusted all along the channel to create daylight even to the farthest reaches of the tunnel where I had landed. How they produced food resources and the delivery system into the channel from outside the Collective's oversight. They spoke with great respect, knowledge, and the only word I could command was delight. They all expressed a very serious delight.

As we walked along the avenue on one side of the channel, I noticed that steps had been carved down to the channel floor every 20 feet or so to allow people to cross back and forth throughout the day and night. Within 200 feet of the opening, a mile at least from where I had landed, I could feel a refreshing breeze blowing upwards from a valley deep below the opening. I could see the minimal light of a dawning day. I then couldn't help but take note of a large crew of people working on a metal net that spanned the width and depth of the channel up to the level of the avenue. Welders had begun to gear up the equipment and the spark and glow of construction was in full force quickly. Other workers used pulleys to raise a section of the net into a fixed position on the other side of the channel, where I saw William talking to a man I would recognize quickly anywhere I went.

William saw me and motioned for me to come across at the same time Doctor waved to welcome me with a smile in his blue eyes that I could see from across the channel. My tour guides hugged me, sharing with me the gratitude of my own life in theirs and the life we now had. I saw the impact of my part. They bid me "good 'den" until then. The Doctor had been teaching I noted. He watched me cross the channel and met me at the top of the steps on the other side, beaming.

The Scottish doctor wrapped me in a bear hug. He bore the same appearance as he had seven years before, bushy mustache and eyebrows, blue eyes alive to every searching detail, and thick, sonorous brogue, and a sense of gravitas about him. "Come with me, Abe," he announced, and we headed to the very opening edge of the channel. He told me in great detail the plan for the next 72 hours. The net, they hoped, would hold the bridge parts that would wash down the channel at 30 mph; the net was engineered and constructed to have tensile strength of bridge construction. It would give, but not break. If it broke, the whole mission would be in ruins.

The breeze picked up as we walked closer to the opening. Within 80 feet of the cliff's edge to the right and the left, rock had been carved out to a distance of 100 yards length on each side. Tables and chairs, awnings over shop entrances to shade people at sundown, sitting areas, and rows and rows of mature plantings and early spring plantings. They had erected a garden area all along the edge of the cliff. Along the wall of the cliff, inner rooms had been carved out. Then an avenue opened up along the "shops." Across the avenue and sitting areas were the gardens that stretched along the whole way from where I stood to the end of the avenue. These people had created a city of life. I could see how they formed a method to capture water that flowed down the channel every day right on schedule. Several people were working at the watering system to guide the sprinklers to cover the ground of new growth.

I could hardly imagine the work necessary to bring so many tons of dirt to the area. I also realized that much of the garden used hydroponic drip methods to water plants that appeared even now to be ready for harvest. They had food year round with their ability to use solar panels to store the sun's rays and keep warmth and light on the soil and hydroponic growth. The Doctor shook me out of my amazement. The beauty of a city on a ledge 1,000 feet from the ground below, the sky and valley out towards the west beyond, a distance filled with trees, mountains, meadows and lakes that they could see but not quite get to. I stood drinking in a whole community living well in liberty and compassion. They had built a temporary place to become home, because home was where these people lived, and yet they had a quest.

Seventy-seven feet from the cliff's edge, the gap between where we stood and the hope of the future, sat another cliff side that was almost level with where we stood, as if thousands of years ago the two sides were connected and had been ripped asunder. Pines and hardwoods covered the plateau on the other side and then appeared to roll downwards quickly to the valley below. The Doctor explained again that the valley below had been reclaimed strip mine land, as William had said, reconstituted by the company that mined there years ago.

The Collective still considered it contaminated and useless because it had been marred by the reprehensible people. The Doctor and others considered it healed by the people that had used it, and so we planned to go to the place of the reprehensible, where we would be forgotten. They wanted to forget us, if we could just make it. "Their apathy of denial will set us free," Doctor said almost to himself it seemed. "We are going to cross on the dawn's wings, Abe," he then said, looking the same way I remembered from years ago when I received the dagger, mission and direction of creation. He had believed a long time before this day came.

"We just need to be ignored a little longer, to walk in their darkness invisible," he said with a wry smile, before calling my name again. I remembered that Doctor knew his Milton. "Abe, there are communities like this all over, in multiple regions using different methods. You will be grateful to know that your sons will join us in this refuge soon, one from north and one from south." I held my breath for a pause as tears came to my eyes with the exhale. I could see back to their childhoods in those seconds. Doctor smiled somberly, giving me time to gather the enormity of what had been coming for years, headed towards a planned result.

"Abe, createds, now people again, thrive here, blessing others and being blessed, living fully amidst life's realities, loving deeply out of gratitude, and leading good lives that have great worth because you and Beatrice are great warriors. You have sweated, risked, bled, cared, grown and loved, even found each other in the midst of this personal titanic struggle. William, likewise, has walked the same path. Sybil will never join him forever now to my heart's sorrow and his," Doctor said, as he looked at William. He went on, "You two have halved your sorrows and doubled your joy by being together," and William nodded somberly as Doctor finished speaking. Then with heavy preoccupation Doctor said, "We will do the same with the others who have sacrificed their children upon the altar of their own egos, too, Abe." Doctor's huskiness of voice and the slump of his shoulders spoke to the never ending sadness of all, of the heart rending grief of diverging from who we were created to become.

William had designed metal stake-like poles that had been secured in deep holes that had been bored into the stone. They planned a cantilever approach.

We would bring the old railroad bridge timbers to the

edge, build a bridge on one side and then swing a right and a left arm out across the 77 feet, floor it with cross timbers and then walk across the short distance, 1,000 feet above the canyon floor. If we could get the timbers to the place, if the net held, if the bridge could be built.

William tapped me on the shoulder and said, "We need to go. The outer-world will be up and going by the time we get back, and I need to show you one more place before we return home." He tucked in his shirt and pushed his glasses to his face. I saw the shirttail begin to come out within two steps as he turned to walk towards the opening. I could not help but smile at this brilliant, quixotic man, even in the midst of the heaviness and sadness of it all.

XXIII

We headed toward the pool where we started, walking quickly, talking and head-nodding to people we passed. "William," I said, as we neared the pool, "how do we get back?" not too thrilled about returning the way we came in. He looked at me bemused and smiled, pushed his glasses up and said, "We go up the staircase carved in the stone that spirals to the surface and out the door on the other side of the grate. It's covered with bushes and forgotten." I looked at him without surprise this time and just shook my head, saying, "You let me go through a terrifying transmorphing just for fun?"

"I wanted you to see how much you have; I went through it again, too. I went through it again with you, Abe," he answered. "We have struggled for years to keep passion and vision, and you have been blessed deeply in all this struggle. I wanted you to see the faith you have gained. Your surrender, and mine, and Bea's and your sons, and thousands of others carry trust, love, courage, the greatest courage of all, the courage of care—care for your people, care for your highest dignity—maximum service. We have not yielded our hearts to a compromise, but yielded them deeply to the intuition of what we have always known, and our presence has been met in it."

At the edge of the spiral steps, an older woman with clear, sharp eyes and a young man with deep eyes handed us bottled gas water, with knowing smiles, and strips of jerky. We climbed the stairs in silence. We left the glass bottles at the top of the steps for reuse, opened the door into the early day and ran towards the thickets that would cross the tracks toward home. On the way, a rumbling blast shocked me from behind. I stopped abruptly and turned towards what I thought could only be an explosion or a blast of a new laser orbiter. I saw nothing but another steam release from the plant. William said with experience, "6:36 a.m., when they open the gates for water from the river and release steam at the same time. Wild sound isn't it? Like an underground blast." He turned to press on, as did I.

William tapped my arm to stop when we came to the tracks near the woods. "Come with me into the thicket. I'll show you the bridge timbers, all stacked neatly years ago and now covered with vines and overgrowth. The creosote has preserved them perfectly and they are heart pine, pure strength of the tree." We moved into the tree line quietly. Birds had come to life in song and movement, beginning their feeding. In the thicket, the scents of spring growth hung in the morning air. In a clearing in the middle of the thicket I could see the stacks of timbers, even through the honeysuckle vines and sticker vines, low hanging limbs of new trees that had grown over the years.

They were 17 by 18 and just as preserved as William had said. He began to talk about the bridge, as much to himself, as to me, "That is what we are going to haul out of here two nights from tonight, all night work to get the beams to the channel by 3:30 and bridging the gap as soon as we can. We will build the cantilever bridge. Two arms we will swing out separately, using metal ropes and pulleys. I will oversee the welding of metal bracings to hold the timbers together, three 30-feet timbers joined by the braces where we will step up in the middle and step down as we go across. That is a long span without under support. We will also place cross beams that we will cut in half, length-wise to lighten the weight on the bridge. If the calculations are correct, we will make it. We will also be pointing a way for others to enter if they can make it."

I took in the size of the mission and looked about intently at the beams. I looked down to consider the work and realized that I was standing in human feces. I stepped back in irritable surprise and began wiping my boots on the weedy grasses. I then noticed lots of piles of feces around where we stood.

William looked somber. He spoke quietly to me, more because of sadness than caution, "Drifters, the Husk people, who wander through here at times, sleeping in the underbrush and vines for shelter. They follow the weather patterns of hot and cold, no longer willing to live differently even when given opportunity. They are the 'forgottens,' spectators of death, the greatest tragedy of all, perhaps. I believe they are the result of reductionistic success. No room for just simply people. It is where the apathy will take any of us—no life in life, no wants, no needs, no strength, as crazy as this sounds, no savagery."

Just as William was saying, "The effect makes the human being irredeemable," I looked over his shoulder to see three people squatting in the vines, staring at us without a sign of awareness. Their eyes weren't hollow as much as they had no energy. William saw me, turned and saw the three in the vines. He didn't stop talking. "I see them, too, Abe, but no one is really there. The creatures themselves offer more hope until the last days of breath even as the created exists in prison. Some of these Huskers were even sons and daughters of professors and achievers; it is not primarily the socioeconomic disadvantage that voids life. It is the character of it."

We stood quietly. I looked up at the sky, clear blue now above me, with some white wispy spring clouds marking the blue, and tears formed in my eyes when I looked back at William. He reflected the same. "Let's go," I said. "Tell me the rest on the way." Neither of us moved. After a moment, William said, "That's what the giant cooker is about. I bring meat to these people when they migrate to this area. If I don't bring it, they either die or eat what's around in the path they follow. Those bowel movements started at my cooker, I reckon," he said turning his head a swift tic to the left as reality and helplessness set in. He pushed his glasses against his nose with the back of his hand. I moved on and he caught up quickly.

As we walked out of the woods, I looked to my left to a man and a woman standing in honeysuckle vines, looking out, eyes without expression; they were like rotting logs or trees waiting to topple with the slightest storm. "May be 30 of them in the woods," William stated as we walked into the open. "May be gone tomorrow or not. Food doesn't even predict their movements."

We moved much more slowly than we had started from the hive, finally exhausted physically and within. William explained the ropes in his warehouse home, the block and tackle, pulleys, torches and welding equipment, concrete bags and onward. We would meet over 100 of the createds, some to move material from the warehouse and the rest of the group would join me in the thicket to begin the operation under a full moon.

We would move six of the largest beams using rope slings placed under the beams and a man on each side to carry the rope end. The group had been coordinating the walking in step for two months. Another group, likewise choreographed in their steps with two people per one tie, would bring crossties to be sawed down the middle of the length of the ties. They would be placed on the cantilever arms after the arms had been secured on the other side of the cliff. If all went well, we would be gone by mid-morning. We would carry enough to start anew, only necessities that fit onto the backs of each person. Much would be left behind; even though we hoped to go back and forth across the bridge several times to gather more things we would need to secure our community quickly. We were now officially pioneers, highly experienced and educated, yet still having to face the elements of the ancients.

Once the beams were placed in the channel, the grate would be cut with torches and moved to open a path to carry the beams on the water into the metal net. The grate would then be welded back as before to cover our disappearance, or at least to block any overt presence that would force the Collective's hand to make a show of us.

As William and I said goodbye at his home, we shook hands and then hugged. We were in this together, drawn by affinity of heart as much as by necessity. I had not needed my knife. Maybe that time could pass and a new era could begin. Maybe our sons could come home to us and live nearby. We could be a family again and share the stories of our quest. We could do it together, build a legacy that would be one of heart and truth, that we would remain awake to what we needed to do, so as not to lose passion and purpose again, where people could have liberty and compassion for others. For certain, my thoughts were no longer just words. They had become living, breathing truths.

"Abe," William said as I turned to go home to Beatrice

and my brother, the last created who would join our region. "My heart breaks open and I'm glad it can relate to the Huskers, though it is a hopeless pain. I want to tell you my favorite paragraph," and he smiled wryly about the use of the word paragraph. "It is sacred to me," he went on, "and was spoken by a president of the United States, during a time when the thought was that a person's private life and public life would not be too far apart, and that lack of separation was called integrity; when statesman still had a common use and politician was considered a term beneath the dignity of the vision for a people. The thinking was not about expectations of perfection, but the expectation of full participation. That is how we knew the good guys from the bad guys, like when we were dreamers as children. Clumsy, truthful, trusting, courageous integrity. You know exactly what I mean."

William pulled his pants up and stared straight at me. "The president said this: 'It is not the critic who counts; not the man who points out how the strong man stumbles, or where the doer of deeds could have done them better. The credit belongs to the man who is actually in the arena, whose face is marred by dust and sweat and blood; who strives valiantly; who errs, who comes up short again and again, because there is no effort without error and shortcoming; but who does actually strive to do the deeds; who knows great enthusiasms, the great devotions; who spends himself in a worthy cause; who at the best knows in the end the triumph of high achievement, and who at the worst, if he fails at least fails while daring greatly, so that his place shall never be with those cold and timid souls who neither know victory nor defeat.'

"You are that man, Abe. I had heard about you from Doctor. He had said as much. When I saw you defeated on that rock wall, I knew that I had run into integrity. You are that man and a proper match for Beatrice." At that, he turned and walked away and I headed home, deeply moved by his words, to share with Bea where we were headed next. We had much to share, plans to make, decisions about what to take. We were leaving our home, but now our home really was wherever we were together. We could take the memories, even though they were so unfinished. I would miss our place, every stone and leaf. The next two days would pass like a few hours and then Josh, Bea and I would go to the hive.

XXIV

Beatrice and I held each other out on the courtyard stones. She had been waiting for me after picking some early spring flowers. No vegetables were ready for picking this early in the spring. I shared as much as I could communicate beyond her having to actually see the hive. I talked her through the plan and the risks. If the Collective found us, they would have to make some kind of example of us, and it would probably be targeted, secretive and deadly. I also told her that our sons were coming into the region. She just sat with her arms around herself and my forehead gently pressed against hers as she softly cried in gratitude. We were tired. And we were ready to go.

After I slept hard for a few hours, we spent the afternoon and the next days letting go. The backpacks were simple; some essentials and a few reminders. Everything else was looking at our history. I reviewed paragraphs; Bea walked through the memories of our lives. We literally were leaving everything behind that had bound us together in a story. Who would tell it; what did it matter? Before our last nightfall we walked down to the cemetery by the backstop to honor the createds that did not make it to life again. They did die free, but still so sadly. I looked up at the great rise where the quest of life began again for me. I looked all about our place from the meadow, and knew that I carried everything I needed in the fullness of my heart. Bea and I looked to each other again and walked silently to the house our last time. The lilies of the field were blooming early I noticed as I walked by the old flowerbed at the edge of the meadow.

The sun went down and darkness settled in; the light of the full moon painted everything outside dark and light. We turned the lights up in the house, and Josh and I made supper while Beatrice packed a second backpack of medical supplies that she knew she would be carrying since Josh would be too weak still to carry anything. Making the journey itself would be his great fortune. We cleaned the dishes and put them away, in hopes that whoever came next might find a place that would offer them something good.

At 9:00 we walked out the back porch door, leaving it unlocked. I heard the squeak of the screen door and the gentle tap it made when it landed in its place. We walked into a night full of stars, darkness, and a full moon. I thought of Washington's bust and the Creation of Man.

After the first mile, Josh asked about Rachel. I smiled and also was embarrassed. I had not even thought to inquire about her or to mention her to Josh. I'm glad he asked; it was a good sign. I had to tell him that I did not see her, but I assured him that if she were there, she would be coming.

After we got to William Williams' place, no spotlight or dog show this time, Bea and I took a quick trip inside the interior before we headed to the thicket. A guide would take Bea and Josh to the hive so Josh could prepare. Bea would be quickly assigned duties by Doctor to triage health concerns and make assignments of accountability for the stronger to assist those who would need extra help across the bridge.

I set to work to start the crews in the movement of beams. It all went off without a hitch; the crews were ready, eager and prepared. We arrived at the channel just before William and his crew. As I looked towards the crew, a woman ran quickly to me when she saw me, one of the welders. She quickly told me that they had found a body tied to the grate, a woman. I ran quickly just as William was coming up behind me. The moment we cast a lantern on the image, I could see that her eyes had been removed from their sockets. At the same time, I recognized the dead woman as Sybil Williams. I heard William groan and turned to see him pushing past everyone to come to her aid. But all he could do was hold her and moan; her body stretched out by the limbs and wired to the grate. She had been dead for hours, if not longer. He said her name over and over. Two people cut the wires and her stiff body fell into his arms. He picked her up and carried her out onto grassy ground, grotesquely because her body had no flexibility in it. She had stiffened horribly into the form in which she had been wired to the grate. I went to him and kneeled on the grass beside them. He kept trying to put her arms near her side, but her body could not be changed.

Death quiet, only nature sounds continued and the steam of the plant. After some time, I knew we had to move. As if on cue, William stood, asked for help with stones, and he asked for a light so we could see. When we moved her body to begin to place stones, Sybil's shirt pulled up above her waist to reveal a 636 written on her stomach in such a way that she would have done it. It was written upside down to us, but right side up if she were writing. William made no other comment but to say, "I get it, Sybil. Thank you."

We gently covered her in a mound of rock. William then ordered everyone to work at their tasks. He told me that she must have "seen" the truth of the Collective, as he made quick quote marks with his hands wide spread. They were no longer permitting any more departures. She must have decided to leave, and she paid a dear price for that decision. "They know we are here," he said matter-of-factly. "We must move now. We have 20 minutes until the water hits. Leave the grate off. It no longer matters. All of us need to go below now. Head to the net. Time is short." And he and I were the last ones down the stairs. Even though I saw his grief, I also saw that something had shifted in my friend.

We made it to the net, arriving just as the beams dropped the 45 feet with a thunderous crashing groan amidst the roar of the water. The water wall ran hard and fast; the beams tumbled and rose in the water in crossed up patterns. All we could do was watch as the first beam and then the whole group at once slammed into the net. The pylons bent towards the opening of the channel. One at the top snapped, and the safety feature of a second catch held, but barely, bending sharply against the weight. The water ran past the beams, the net held, and a chorus of shouts went up. William and I remained quiet. I watched him. He was focused but gone, and I understood. I knew I needed to watch him.

The crew began to separate the beams and place them in their stations. Doctor told William that he would handle all the crews, for him to concentrate on engineering only. William quickly agreed, knowing he had little else to offer. The holes were drilled quickly with a massive drill powered by a compressor that required two people to operate. The first beam slid smoothly over the metal pole that would act as a spin point and grounding point once the arms were hoisted out over the cliff's edge. The welders had made the sleeves exactly to William's specs. They fit perfectly. The pulleys were activated after everyone was in place and the arms were maneuvered across the space in a matter of minutes. They thudded into place just as planned. The crossties were cut and placed across the arms and secured by people of such dexterity and lightness of step I had never seen.

Doctor silenced everyone after very well deserved cheers subsided. He asked William if the moving could commence, to which he waved a forward motion. Over a thousand people moved with grace and care across a thousand-foot drop without incident. Josh indeed had found Rachel. Rather, Rachel had found Josh. They had already crossed. Doctor finally went and then Beatrice and I crossed. I called William to come on. He busied himself with something. I ran back half way across the bridge, noting that William was doing something to one of the gas engines. I called him. He turned and ran hard toward me, dangerously so. He was almost to me in the middle of the bridge when a plume of fire shot up into the sky with a repercussion that knocked me down and William too. He landed beside me with a hard grunt of pain. I jumped up, grabbed him and we landed on the other side next to Bea's outstretched arms at her feet.

The bridge remained steady, but the rocks on the other side began to crumble and slide. Then the lights that had shown into the channel and the hive went out as the hive caved in at its entrance. The bridge beams then cracked on our side where it had been secured, snapped its moorings and then the whole bridge began the descent of 1,000 feet. I reached to the ground and pulled William Williams up to my chest and growled into his face, "You fool, others could have come across! Others could have come across! You foolish selfish goat of a man!" Bea pulled my arm back as William Williams slumped to the ground and put his head between his knees. "They took Sybil!" he screamed and then he began to weep. Just as quickly as I had grabbed him by his shirt, I now kneeled to the ground, putting my arms around him as he wept against me for a long time. I told him that,

"Sybil took Sybil, yet her last gesture was towards you."

I leaned towards Bea, who watched us both within an arm's length. I reached out as I rose to her and gently released William who had come to a rest and needed to sit. "When you're ready, William, come on towards the campsite. Doctor will need to see you for tomorrow's work. OK?"

"Abe," William said slowly, "I know what I did was not what you would have done. I put your life at a terrible risk, and I am already sorry. Had you not cared about me, you would not have come back across the bridge. Thank you. No more people were going to be coming across. Sybil let us know that tonight. She somehow wrote 636 on her stomach before her death in the hope, I know, that I would see it and know how to assimilate the message. That 636 is the 6:36 a.m. schedule when the plant creates the greatest amount of noise. I figured the Collective had decided to give us until 6:36 to get out before they made it impossible for anyone else to leave or for us to come back."

Just as I was slowly grasping the man's brilliance and forming other questions, a rumble on the other side shook the rocks and I realized a second explosion was coming as rocks blew out through the channel cave-in William had caused. They spilled forward down the canyon depths, fire and smoke following with more and more rock until nothing but dust and smoke began silently to drift away in the morning breeze. I looked at William who had just glanced down at his watch. He said, "6:39 a.m. Thank you, poor Sybil.

I will always love you. I understand."

William then looked up at me and said, "So I helped them build their lake. That blast was intended to create a lake for them. I'm sure the new gift of the Collective to advance the cause of good for all of us. We might just have been downstream collateral damage. We planned to be out by mid-morning. We are ahead of schedule. Their blast could have blown over here and perhaps killed more of us. I set an initial blast to counter, I hoped, what would have been worse without that defense. Sybil saved us. We would almost certainly be in the middle of crossing or preparing to cross when they detonated their explosives. Her cryptic message depended on her trust of me to be who she never really could not love.

No more water will run down the channel. Seven days a week, millions of gallons of water will be held by the dam I helped them manufacture. They will claim credit for enriching the people with a new leisure area. I only regret the Huskers, and those imprisoned createds who died without freedom, and that my warehouse of interests will be flooded in the valley and never be put to use again. I'm grateful for Sybil. She died free. I hope she did not suffer horribly before she was put to death.

Based upon how they control the water flow, your home will become a lakeside bed and breakfast or some important Collective member's new house, I assume." He then laughed a little snort while he looked at the ground with his arms in front of him and one hand clasping a wrist as if in thoughtful repose now. The man had known grief for years and it would never leave him. But for a moment, he had rich completion of a dream.

"But who," I said, as William looked up quickly towards me and said, "Not who, what."

Bea put her hand on my shoulder and face against my chest. I held her against me for a moment, and then looked into her eyes. We had made it for now. We slowly moved down the ridge towards the camp where Doctor would be. I heard the first notes of William's flute behind us. Bea and I smiled to each other. He would join us at his own pace.

I gazed down into the valley where we were headed and knew for sure at that moment that we humans never change. We cannot have a utopian anything. We will always need contracts. A person's word would always have consequences, whether they keep it or not. And covenant is the most sacred word that exists. William and I would always be friends, but the best any of us ever become is in our ability to admit our humanity, surrender to how we are made and seek help. What makes a human most noble is accepting that we are created. It is the origin of true creativity. That acceptance may be most important of all.

I would always persevere. I had fallen into the culvert years ago, and now I was going to finish what I had been assigned to do.

We would soon see our sons.

WAR OF LOVE

I

Suffocation of the past has tendrils reaching for me out of a gray jungle that has sounds in it, quiet sounds nearby, like clicking and digging of creatures I cannot see. Echoed in the distance slight remembrance of screams now muffled by how far away they are, too far to be able to do anything about them. And the clicking makes me know I cannot sit, lie or sleep. Once a tendril catches me and pulls... once a clicking sound I see... once a digger shows itself... a tendril, a clicker, a digger... I'm trapped again in all the anguish of waiting in pain, not sounding, not ending, no destination, waiting in survival, getting through, enduring the close of everything I do not want and yet close slides closer as the only direction inertia takes, down to the point hiding the truth takes us all.

Awful is that my people of my past, my own blood, hide here, always one mirage from reach, an echo gone behind a rise I can't get over. Freedom's cry I cannot not believe and yet illusion in my hands seeps through my pores and moves towards the last place that breathes love inside me and is still shocked daily with adrenaline to believe, knowing nothing will be different but the race to move illusion with the hope that I still thankfully cannot not believe.

If I find them, and I have many times, standing still with my eyes open and breathing with anticipation of a tendril grasping, a clicker moving quickly with a snapping so fierce and burning that my scream will drive me crazy too, and if I slide into crazy, we are all gone, maybe all gone anyway.

I stand ready, looking at them, suggesting with my eyes what I know I'm looking into but they will not look because blindness allows illusions and deafness allows pretending and blocking connection allows blending into the clicking until caught somewhere in a place where the screams come from, but if caught there, no return—not one single return in all my years, and they are piling up like rocks. Weeds grow amidst the pile, making even getting to the beginning harder and more easily ignored, forgotten, and just simply there like bad dirt covered by years of sawgrass, scrawling Bermuda begging along the ground, grasping at spots where sludge hasn't painted death to anything reaching.

The scream I think—no—I know because I remember— has consequences of the fractured bones, scattered white bones, enough to see life was where I stand and is now scattered invisible but for being familiar enough with their shape and whiteness to say what it was.

The scream makes isolation, uselessness, not despair, it's the over and over that we cannot nor are we born able to believe, yet it happens and is real and if we don't awaken and come with me, we, we now... the word we, I was made for and have to escape to live because it has become poison and if breathed will incinerate any vestige that decency can be more than fakery.

Not despair because that can be a resting place. Not despair, that being no pain, impossible in me anyway. Never could get there, making me a freak in illusion, an anomaly, and if spoken in the other places a freak to break up decency that remains decent by promising to forget. I'm a freak either way. Love is a freak

No scream, that becomes the over and over again. No sleep, which marks disappearances and never knowing illusions that is real now from insanity that is not real but comforts.

I stand, looking with my eyes into eyes that have meaning in them but declare words that tell me to stand still, just stand still. If I do even one more, one more slice of time that marks itself with heartbeats not watches and I am slipped into and could be an echo in my silence fast. I cannot do so. Love is a freak.

I'm going now. Backing up while looking, now seeing them reach out for a grasp, hands out, leaning over and over until like fog rolling over something, creeping low to the earth, envelopes the reach and they are gone. I ache with the disaster of blame, looking hard into the fog until I say I made it up and I will keep the secret and it will be like movements of a memory. Again I watch but my touch has no movement to shift or *bring to awake anyone. I move on, not like dreams but like the life you and I walk in every day of sickness and health, rich and poor, in good times and bad, where savagery lurks just below the promise. I'm backing away like moved without my own feet though I am, I am, I am, I am, I am, I am doing it.*

In decency now, sweet decency where I don't like much; my watchfulness looks through my eyes, a wolf watching for movements of clickers, diggers, teeth and air moving out mouths that have poison on the breath. Careful, slow; hold love back. Love is a freak. I miss the place I just backed out to walk on flat grass that smells like summer cuttings and see flowers that make me ache inside with a thing called good that I have never been willing or able to shed. I am not a snake. I cannot shed. I don't want to. This has saved me and prayer to the moon, before I go back into a house where dark corners walked by and smoke trapped against the ceiling, ghost-like from mouths that will not say anything.

I pray towards the moon, the light in the gray sky that gets black and makes the infinite pretty. The moonbeams spread out and the rock against my back has the slightest warmth from me, or it still lingering about me while I am a spot; I believe because the scent of Invisible who is whispering near somewhere my ache tells me is, please. The moon tells, the caterpillar tells, the blade of grass tells, the dirt where toy car tracks mark play tell, the pumpkins tell, as do the zinnias, and carrots with green sprouts on their heads tell and climbing a fence to go into the next field tells and the tree that stands on the rise in the field over the fence by itself marked against the horizon by the moon light in the black, the tree tells. And the fescue and broomsedge under its limbs tell. Romance like pearls rolling down a piece of oak lumber; follow them for they tell that it is all true.

But dogs drink water with maggots; rain-soaked paste of chunks, maggots make it move, sitting rats on edge stick spear-like snouts in paste, yellowed teeth and white with gnawing, pink clawed toes, whiskers nasty with vermin-like vermin pasted to sides sleek combed hair—quick to dart; dogs, lazy-sick waiting on rats, not even dogs---no newspaper, no hearth, no names but to remind them all with ears still flat that name is only that, rousing flinching muscles to nothing left that happened.

Rain with thunder warming muffled hopes in water deep enough to tap on the top and seen upside down. Stay down, stay down, warm in the tapping, faster, harder. Lightning, lightning. Rise from the water. Clap, shake, boom, light water. Grass on feet. On a knee to pray, diving in, down, down, bubbles, thunder, sitting on the edge. More of the invisible came keeping on of where the pearls come from and the pumpkins, trumpet vines blooms and nighthawks swoosh, whip-o-wills cry from lonesomeness I had to look up in a book because no one sees where the sound comes from. It would see a bird not the twilight around the call when the woods begin to snap quietly and the last sparrow taps a twig settling into cedar greens nestled in twigs and moss. Little houses of quiet where

children whisper trusting in the dark like ZuZu's petals, say-
ing, "Fix it, Daddy," and he lies.

Drink cold sulfur water, turn around, one winged insect
crawls down the shaved poplar plank, then another. Up the
wall more of them, in and out of rotted crevices in redeemed
wood. More and more. I move the sheetrock by digging and
mounds of them are moving the whole building and they
won't stop.

How am I whole? I trace the Invisible with a finger again
in the dark and tell no one. I ask the Invisible from a place
where the whip-o-will protects its eggs if I would have to
wrestle the savage on dull mats, whose dull eyes made them
copy caged animals that kept being told they could do what
they wanted cause they were free; they were not free. Savaged
school with little kids who could hear the sparrows.

The Invisible would say, "No" or almost say, "It will be
OK" and I would keep begging anyway because there really,
really was not another place to go below concrete that remitted
nothing under it. I don't even want the Invisible to be named
near the retarded animals. So I double my fist when pushed
and wait for the blows where I stand the ground on creaking
bent floors that will be thrown into the dump and bulldozers
push the memories underground, growing crabgrass over the
fill hole of worn down dirt.

But I remember. The Invisible knows I know and we are
quiet, real quiet in a place where covering the light is smart,
acceptable and allows the decent into the country club and

no one dares for but a second, but there are seconds, to look too long or take a breath too deep to exhale the truth that will indicate what they know because it will throw them forward with their legs pulled out from under them. They will be dragged by tendrils with fingers bloodied fast grabbing at razor sharp corals that cut them to pieces hanging on for a life they would not breathe the truth about. Spit burning clickers' jaws mash into diggers grabbing at the forefront to where you bet you could deny.

I know, now, not to be fast to look towards the sparrow or speak of its mystery quickly because it makes rumblings in the decent and the floor goes with them. Still, stand, can't lie down here, either. Not yet. Decent. Descent. Remember. Cling.

Damned ooze; there is no word for seepage moving into swept place. Creeping like thickened syrup leaving all kinds of time to torture in the inevitable fact that this night, where the moonbeams streak the ground, the darkness with it, is not sweet enough but still says cling until the drops of rain fill a cup to swallow cool butterflies' colors tasted like life to last a little longer with the truth quietly tucked into a sparrow's nest for the night so that I can stand while I rest, not lie down while I sleep even when the dreams come that beg the Invisible to make it stop. Oh, Invisible, I stand resting at the tree in darkness where the pearls roll down rough-hewn oak.

I like the face I have never seen, who kept me whole. I saw the star I am so alive with and still trace my steps on the light that comes in water and wings and the sequence of wav-

ing promise in between. I am going now. Love is a freak. Decent; descent. Go to bed, stepping down blue stoned hallways,
cut stone walls slow path beating blood vessels slowing down
the pulse of hope for today again clung to not one sparrow
stayed. The life beyond the blood still reaches me with strands
under my shoulders that let me rest while standing a night
lived only with the life beyond doing the breathing because the
walk down the hallway slowed the pulse to nothing.

In the standing through the chimes of the night the life
beyond the pulse starts not decent and others are there while
no one speaks the truth that each one stands in, can't lie down
to die, and knows no rest but this that happens now will be the
respite and it only comes with sweat.

My breath comes easy running at a pace quickened by
early night in fall's fog. A sweet one in which a shower of rain
came on a warm day, then coolness of evening started, so that
drips of rain still waited to fall from leaves that did likewise
soon to be about the ground that waited for the covering. I
ran dreaming of valor; by running, I could reach it. Past a
row of seven trees planted near the curb by the street I ran
down. I run down the trodden mud path beside them, and
feel the absorption of sweat blending me into the warm fog,
and drops of rain waiting with the leaves that do the same.
My breath is wet and pulls in the coolness of evening and I
believe in the yes because I sweat and breathe and push, and I
am free in the dream that where I run I will find a place that
white clover blooms in patches cool to the touch. When I stop,

steam rises from heat into the coolness of night, sweat trickles down my face, feet squishing in winter's Bermuda. Invisibility rests within me and around me, while I watch the lights of cars passing, the electric lighted clock down the street, street lights and the short walk on moonbeams and pavement where even the discarded pebbles pushed up on the pavement have a marked recognition with the eyes and the drips into the storm culvert get their due with my ears before fading into the invisible I now get to walk in. And it is so lonely, and I don't know this word in my mouth or the word taboo. The invisible Invisible I know knows the words I have not spoken yet, but I write right now from where the words wander. I'm all myself blended, gone, and invisible but to the Invisible, some blip of heat that makes tragedy absolute because the reality can twist the truth into the comfort of the invisible in which only the Invisible breathes vestiges of standing so something will happen that does not, but I cling. It is coming now; dazed into re-entering the decent. Descent into words I didn't even know, not knowing the words so I can be invisible another way.

But my eyes see. I did not even know they were seeing everything. Last of the truth I took in before the heavy jacket goes on and waiting in pretending the attack won't come tonight, where the lights of the fireflies rising and floating in the night go. Curling their lanterns about the air, tiny worlds weaving recognition that the order underneath and pulsing claims romance, unstoppable.

II

By the creek of clear water that roars fast over rounded stones at aways away a cool pool forms by gritty sand underneath small trees with wide waxy green leaves. Soft flowers poof out from the branches. Dogwoods up away from the pool of quiet make pearls roll down oak lumber in browns and tall trees that disappear because they are so many the same color. The world becomes a universe and the place rolls out into the safety of butterflies in a hospital.

A child moves along the soft grit of sand, squishing mountain water up on bare feet with the sun on his back and hair pierced by the sun snapping light back to memories of what was made to be and somewhere slipped in a storm down a culvert of underground missings.

Quiet, so quiet in the middle of the silence of the woods of mountains where the pool settles and butterflies with black wings and deep spectrums in circles of color so profound that the eyes cry in wonder that so much could land on wings that break so easily, leaving scars of dust on fingers that just want to fix their broken flight. He and I gather them up and make rooms on the gritty sand, lots of small rooms for dead butterflies, arrange and build with sticks slatted roofs that cover their resting place, with sticks crossing the tops of rocks that sit on gritty sand. Seven butterfly rooms. Quiet places where they sleep in lying down, and sit and rest, but they want move again when the wind chime tinkles sad-like, by the sound it says so, and breaks between the chiming are silent and that is where the awe comes from to make peace in the sound and in between.

So quiet at the pool, even the child's breath is quiet. He does not even know how quiet and the hum comes so still that if you have eyes and ears with silver lines that wrap around the beating of blood making me care, then you would break wide open. You would tell him to with you, to bring the butterflies and the pearls; the sparrow will go first to meet him on a ledge in the morning of an ancient city of stones, waking up with the sun and bread that has as much smell as hope coming from a warm oven. Pumpkin vines grow up bricks and pumpkins will rest on shingles of a house ever, not magic but real as the hum makes things live. They live like jewels kept in velvet memory places that can't be kept out too long because storms will wash them into a culvert and then all has to go there to keep the jewels.

But he does not hear, still so close to living in the attachment, not knowing that clinging to the pool's edge quietly making rooms for butterflies' rest marks one of the last resting places before the roar moves in taking everything but what beats in blood with the Invisible, connected now by a humming.

Humming so soft that eyes and ears, like you know, with silver lines coming from the pulse strum quietly tears that the roar washes over without even a nothing so full with the blindness it is already. Humming breaks you wide open and you reach for him to come with you before the roar overcomes and washes everything you and he know to be true to the descent into the decent as the best there is in suffocation of pretending or the mashing dance of apes growling yellow teeth and hairy pads squalling to avoid the electrical torment of breaking wide open with tears.

He looks up from the butterflies' phosphorescent blue circles into the deeps of the dogwoods and tears of not knowing that the null pursued with a roar so loud that it blotted everything to silence rolled down the face of everyone who could even have one glimpse of electrical torment of memory when the hum still came quietly in the evening.

Somewhere else the roar receded to, somewhere now the hum from over the rainbow where all the truths lived knitted together, with eyes open, became separate and as unique as one simple circle of phosphorescent blue. Bluebirds fly promise me you do hang, that this descent makes blindness sight and deafness hearing while stillness makes that a very breathable crying lie.

There's no place like home, not any place, awakening softly to the quiet of the unspoken—that it leaves and goes to the culvert: and standing, not lying down or sitting, to watch for clickers acid gnarling bites and diggers claws, the echoing screams do not come to thee. I'm going now. Love is a freak, not letting go, following the pearls and the standing because anything else love rejects so it itself raises up the descent.

The pulse deafens him, now a roar to him because he sees and now knows the burning fire of hope unvanquished within himself that cannot rest in sparrows' lairs or butterflies' dens but now in all the pure blood of hope, booming now louder, louder making pain the sensor of life and wishing that it would stop, but it cannot even in the midst of the stench of pus covering anything that reaches from itself to what it is made for. He knows with tears that the blue of the circle, the blip of light at night from a flying piece of summer and the petal from the slightest missed branch on the smallest missed bloom that settles in the pus will be the call to screaming war.

And he cries now watching from eyes behind stone, the one in the dust in the corner of the yard hemmed in by trees, toy truck pushed along the ground in tracks of magic for future creation; the sky moves up to see a bomber and the windows on the house are dark in daylight; then, right then, that very moment he sees and now we see through eyes behind stones the absolute crush of broken hearts and the terror of pearls rolling down oak planks that others won't follow, so there we all are. Descent into the decent calls out the clickers and the diggers, gnarling harsh spits on yellow fangs moving quickly like dashing shadows that crash noises until time to growl at their cuttings.

And then the doors shut where the pearls have small sweet flames coming from their tops, cushioned in sparrows' down and butterfly dust, where pumpkin seeds and trumpet vine blooms circle the feast of light and June bug wings still glisten green there and a white clover chain make scent; I can smell the hope smoke puff up because the ones in the room, one or a multitude, just simply blew out the sacrifice of life and *still the firefly flickered one more time before smeared across the table top in the dark, leaving a trail like a comet in a tiny universe that crosses the darkness and is gone. Love is such a freak, wrested by the descent into the decent and stomped into pissed-oil by the apes of blood lust. And still we, you and I, if you have the slightest memory—and if you have come this far, you do—we go with the rains washed into the culverts without a fight because our courage has tears of pursuit wrapped around our hope buried in the memory place that we could not exile even when we knew self-hatred would be the reward of revolution until the grief that came with the valor's limp let us walk the long walk home to the war in which not one of us gives up.*

Love is a freak and I stand still unable, unable, so unable to do anything else for I have seen thee the Invisible visible in the whispers of the quiet things that move in unconscious rolls to touch the memories of anyone of us warriors of the pearls who can do nothing but follow the pearls down planks of oak to the collision that splits the decent descent and cries louder than thunder for a war of departure and sanctuary to anyone who cannot but lean into the yes. I cannot stop going the way of the Invisible. A war of love, o' bluebirds fly, o' yes, and soar with eagles to destinations that the heart of the Invisible called us to remember before we were born. Will we? Please. I'm leaving now. Love is a freak. I am a freak. My face matches the color of my eyes, breaking me from the descent into decent or rat snouts' rage.

Refuge for them. Replenishment for them; redemption; I cry. Make room.

Cool fescue spread below the breezing wind that brushes the harp strings of sedge bristles touched golden by the sun setting low as the last of fall's light kisses a darkening horizon goodnight. Grackles fly away to where the Invisible calls them home. I hear their wings wisp over so low and gone, and I know that I am too.

THE END

ABOUT THE AUTHOR
CHIP DODD

———

Chip Dodd, PhD, is a teacher, trainer, author, and counselor, who has been working in the field of recovery and redemption for over 30 years. It is the territory in which people can return to living the way we are created to live—where we can move from mere survival to living fully, from isolation to loving deeply, and from controlling to leading others well.

In 1996 he founded The Center for Professional Excellence (CPE) in Nashville, TN; a multidisciplinary treatment center for licensed professionals with addiction, depression, burnout, anxiety, and other behavioral problems.

With his clinical experience, love of storytelling, and passion for living fully, Chip developed a way of seeing and expressing one's internal experience called the Spiritual Root System™. It expresses the essential heart of human beings and gives practical tools to live fully, love deeply, and lead well.

Chip founded Sage Hill: A Social Impact Organization with the mission to utilize the Spiritual Root System™ in helping people see who they're made to be, so they can do what they're made to do.

ALSO BY CHIP DODD:

———————

The Voice of the Heart: A Call to Full Living
The Perfect Loss: A Different Kind of Happiness
Live Fully, Love Deeply, & Lead Well Meditations

———————

FIND MORE AT CHIPDODD.COM